Jesus and Menachem

A Historical Novel in the Time of the Second Temple

SIEGFRIED E. VAN PRAAG

TRANSLATED FROM THE DUTCH BY LEWIS C. KAPLAN

TRANSLATION COMPLETED BY PIETER UYS

ARRANGED, EDITED AND COLLATED BY KALMAN J. KAPLAN

WIPF & STOCK · Eugene, Oregon

JESUS AND MENACHEM
A Historical Novel in the Time of the Second Temple

Wipf and Stock Publishers
199 W. 8th Ave., Suite 3
Eugene, OR 97401
www.wipfandstock.com

ISBN 13: 978-1-62032-701-2
Manufactured in the U.S.A.

Originally published under Siegfried E. Van Praag. Jezus en Menacheem. Roman Wereld- Bibliotheek. Amsterdam- 1951-Antwerpen

Jesus and Menachem

I would like to dedicate this translation in the name of my father Lewis C. Kaplan (Yehuda Lev ben Moshe HaKohen) to his grandson and my son Daniel Lewis Kaplan (Daniel Lev ben Kalman Hillel HaKohen),who is named after him. Lew Kaplan never had the chance to know Dan, who was born eleven years after he died, but my late mother, Edith Saposnik Kaplan, also an author, made sure that Dan knew his grandfather. This is "grandpa Lew's" present to you, my son.

—Kalman J. Kaplan
(Kalman Hillel ben Yehuda Lev haKohen)

Contents

Foreword

THIS TRANSLATION HAS A long and fascinating history. It was begun but not completed in the early 1950s by my late father, Lewis C. Kaplan, from an acclaimed novel in Dutch, *Jesus and Menachem* by Siegfried Emanuel van Praag, the prolific Dutch-Jewish writer of more than sixty books. Van Praag was born to Jewish parents and was the youngest of three sons. Apart from his Dutch and Jewish cultural roots, Siegfried's education also introduced him to French language and culture. He pursued French studies at the Universiteit van Amsterdam, after which he became a lecturer at the Hogereburgerscholen in Purmerend. The rise of Nazism may have prompted a move to Brussels in 1936, and was definitely the reason why Van Praag and his family left the continent for England in 1940. In London he worked for the Dutch and Belgian radio programmes of the BBC. The war and the *shoah* made a considerable impression on Van Praag, and his consequent preoccupation with Jewish culture and identity—specifically Dutch Jewish culture and the newly formed country of Israel—can be noted in the published works that follow this period.

Lew Kaplan, a published translator in America of Brazilian and later Dutch novels was struck by the importance and beautiful prose of this novel when he first read it. He translated a large part of the novel and outlined the remainder while he was searching for a publisher. In a letter addressed to a "Mr. Weinstock" on July 25, 1952, my father described the book as containing "profound discussions, beautiful language, and deeply moving dramatic scenes." My father died of complications from childhood rheumatic fever in 1958 before he was able to find a publisher. The uncompleted translation lay dormant in my possession for many years. In the late 1980s, I met Dr. Herman M. van Praag, then chief of psychiatry at Albert Einstein College of Medicine, in the course of my work in suicide and in psychology and religion. I recognized his last name as the same as the author of this book, Siegfried van Praag, and inquired as to whether the two van Praags were related. Herman M. van Praag informed me that Siegfried was his uncle and was then living in Belgium. As it turned out, I was going to a conference that year in Brussels and had the honor to meet Siegfried. He remembered my father's work from years past, but had not realized my father died, and thought he had lost interest in the project. Many years after the work originally began, I was able to finally sign a contract in 2004 with the children of Siegfried, Dr. Herman J. van Praag and Dr. Ganna J. Ottevaere-van Praag, to complete this project. It has taken me many years to finish my father's translation, and I have now done so with the wonderful help of Pieter Uys, a talented student of mine from South Africa. Thanks are also due to Larry ten Harmsel for his resolving of certain translation inconsistencies.

And of course this book is important in placing Yeshua of Nazareth in the context of the Judaism and Israel of his time. While fictional, this book introduces the character of Menachem in an attempt to deepen the understanding between the Jewish people and the Christian world to foster an intelligent understanding of a Biblical approach towards life.

Kalman J. Kaplan

Preface

COMPLETED IN 1947, *JESUS and Menachem* generally reflects the knowledge available at that time regarding the life of Yeshua of Nazareth during the period of Second Temple Judaism. Since then, historical research and textual analysis have contributed significant contextual insight and revealed contradictions in the earliest sources that remain unresolved. For example, a reputable corpus of scholarship suggests that the negative stereotyping of the Pharisees (and hence of the Jewish people throughout the Christian era) was invented and the conflict between Jesus and the Pharisees exaggerated or even manufactured to facilitate the spread of the new religion throughout the Roman Empire.

Some historians even hold that Yeshua was a Pharisee himself, albeit a messianic one, and have highlighted the difference between the Hebrew "Moshiach" and the Greek "Christos." Prominent experts have also pointed to the tolerance of the Pharisees for messianism, illustrated by the great Pharisaic teacher Gamaliel, among both Jews and non-Jewish God-fearers (Noahides) among them. They have also raised serious doubts about the Judas Iscariot narrative and the exoneration of Pontius Pilate, who crucified thousands of Jews in his term as Procurator of Judea, for the murder of Yeshua. They also raise questions about the involvement of the Sanhedrin and the true teaching of Yeshua.

The letters I. N. R. I. (*Iēsus Nazarēnus, Rēx Iūdaeōrum*), denoting "Jesus the Nazarene, King of the Jews" at the top of the cross on which Yeshua was crucified, provide compelling evidence that his offense in Roman eyes was political and not religious—specifically his claim to kingship of Israel, a correlate of messianism. In other words, Jesus's messianic claim and that of the Nazarenes was no real religious threat to the Pharisees but was seen as a political threat both to Rome and her Sadducee allies to Rome's occupation of Judea.

Finally, the character Paul (Saul) of Tarsus occurs in this fictional text as a contemporary of Yeshua—a scenario explicitly denied by the existing theological sources. It has become increasingly clear that Paul never met Yeshua, was not part of the Jerusalem Nazarene Church led by James and Peter, and only entered the picture later, as a rival claimant, after his reported vision of Jesus on the road to Damascus. It is likely that new scholarship emerging in the reborn state of Israel and elsewhere will shed even further light on the emergence of Christianity from Judaism in the Second Temple period.

Kalman J. Kaplan

BOOK ONE

The Cross-Conversation of Youth

1

ONCE AGAIN MENACHEM SET out alone. Although his parents had never lacked a circle of friends, no one had yet come close to seeking his friendship. Wealth attracted only adults, not the young, he thought. Especially here in this dump of Nazareth in the middle of Galilee where his father had moved for the sake of business. Menachem had not fared much better in Jerusalem. True, children had been welcome in his home and sometimes he went out with groups of companions. But he also felt, as it were, unaccustomed to other children and so he remained alone.

Outside the town and the dirty grey embrace of its bumpy streets, Menachem sat down on a stone, thinking that he really had no goal. The road was like a line of yellow powder that ran down to the plain which stretched out in the distance, green with crops and vegetation.

There the forests lifted their small shaggy backs. From the middle of the plain rose Mount Tabor. The mountain was full of the secret powers of the earth and more inscrutable than a human body which one can cut open. Menachem loved the spaciousness of that Galilean landscape.

At that moment a group of boys appeared from the village on the road which led northwards to godless Tiberias. Menachem was frightened and abashed. He wore a richly stitched mantle and sandals with silver thongs. His head was covered by a luxuriously embroidered red cap. His parents were rich people and he was ashamed of it. The boys remained standing before him.

"Ho, Jerusalemite," they jeered, "did you steal those clothes again? Surely, your father is a tax collector for the stinkers." "Hey, Judean, what are you doing here? Did you come to spy for the great Idolator, or for the old greybeards of the Sanhedrin? We smell of cow dung; tonight you will stink too. What will your mother say to that?"

"Come on, fellows, let's chase him," yelled another ringleader. "Ho, Jerusalemite, get up! Aren't you going to stand up? We'll teach that rich boy to run once. Then tonight he can say at home he had a peasant behind his ass."

They began to look for the numerous small pebbles which lay everywhere before them on the road.

"Say, fellows, I've got a swell idea. Let's stone him. Yea, let's stone the little sissy from Jerusalem."

The first throw hit him. Menachem felt a pain in his shinbone where the sharp edge of the stone had cut open his skin.

"Are you mad? Hands which stone will be palsied; and hands which have stoned an innocent will rot away!"

"There he goes spoiling our fun again. Go to the rabbis, woodchopper; there you can learn to split letters."

But it was remarkable that none of the boys ventured to cast another stone at Menachem, who with large questioning eyes continued to gaze at the strange lad who had hindered the others from completing their pastime.

"We are going to look for more boys. Come along, Yeshua, we are turning down another road."

Yeshua, as the others called him, was a thin, poorly dressed boy with a grave demeanor. His eyes were full of power. Sometimes that power appeared to pull inward, other times to flow out. His mouth was drawn with generous strokes. Nevertheless, there was something grim, almost indignant about that youthful countenance. A very docile companion he could not have been.

This Yeshua had magnificent hair, neither brown nor black, but like precious rosewood his locks flashed from brown to black and from black to brown.

This then was Yeshua, who had been unwilling to stone another lad simply because he came from somewhere else and in the course of his childhood years had become somewhat different from other boys.

"What do you see in me, Yeshua, that you have helped me?" asked Menachem, who had now gotten to his feet.

"Nothing unusual," replied Yeshua quietly, continuing to stand before him. "One of the many who should not be hit, but who, nevertheless, are struck."

They did not resemble each other; the boy from Nazareth looked healthier. The Jerusalemite had black hair combed backwards, which encircled the back of his head, and ears like a hood. Here and there where the light bored an opening it glittered. He had a dull sallow skin, delicate hands, withered mouth, with large questioning eyes which lay forever ready for affection. Menachem felt himself drawn to this first child of the poor who had been willing to speak to him without spitting on him.

He loved the poor people, the dust of the highways and the roughness of the ground. Once in Jerusalem when he had been younger and could not yet understand the distinction between homesickness and death, he had lain down in the filthy street with his best clothes and nestled his head against the stones plastered over with camel dung.

Thereupon, one of his father's servants had gone outside, picked the child up roughly and carried him into the house. It was the only time his mother had allowed anyone to spank him.

"Who are you, boy?" asked Menachem.

"I am Yeshua ben Joseph the carpenter, and you?"

"I am Menachem ben Gedalia. My father is the merchant from Jerusalem, he whom they call Marcus Mercator," answered Menachem. "Will you go home with me?"

"Why not?" said Yeshua. "Where another has set foot, I too can enter."

"Yes, but we are rich people."

"That is not your fault."

The boys walked together. Menachem could not tear away his eyes from Yeshua but the latter paid no attention to his new comrade.

"Does your father love you?" Menachem asked him abruptly.

Yeshua looked at him. "I do not ask myself that question. Do you want me to put the same query to you?"

Menachem nodded. "My father does not love me. He does not think me a worthy successor. I don't want to be a merchant. He also says I ask too many questions."

Yeshua remained silent.

"Do you mean to say it doesn't matter what your father thinks about you?" resumed Menachem after a pause. "Do you really think so?"

"I believe it," said Yeshua.

Menachem shook his head.

"But it does matter, it matters very much. If you have everything, you never know what the next one needs and that's important. It is not very pleasant at home when your father does not love you. My father thinks I can become dangerous. Are you dangerous also, Yeshua?"

"I am dangerous too. Blessed are they who expose themselves to danger, for they bring blessings."

"You speak just like the prophets. But no one is a blessing to everyone."

Yeshua surveyed Menachem thoughtfully.

"That is hair-splitting."

"No, it is not, Yeshua. If I were a blessing to my mother I would be sitting with the rabbis, with Gamaliel in Jerusalem, but then I would not be a blessing to my father who wants me to be a merchant."

Finally they reached the rich house of the merchant Gedalia ben Sirach, the Jerusalemite. It lay at the end of a path which led north from the village of Nazareth and had formerly belonged to a rich Roman who had withdrawn into beautiful Galilee. Yeshua, who had never set foot in a rich man's house before, was not disconcerted by this at all and stepped boldly inside as though he were in his father's shop.

"I shall bring you to my mother," said Menachem. "If you wish to make her happy, pretend you're my friend."

Entering the atrium they came to a large oblong room where a broad stone table stood on curved ebony legs. On the shelves on the walls stood a row of brightly colored plates and dishes. Against the wall of the great room a seven-branched candelabrum blazed on top of an ivory table. The stone floor was richly overlaid with dark carpets. It was a room which seemed to absorb the light in waves, and to give it back only here and there on the edge of some gaudy metal leaf.

"Here we eat," said Menachem. "Come." He lifted a hanging carpet in the corner of the oblong room, and he and Yeshua entered a dark corridor. Only by feeling one's way could one ascertain that this small space was sealed here by walls and there by yielding tapestries. But before they could push one of the carpets aside they heard groans, followed a moment later by a sob.

"That is my mother," said Menachem. "She is unhappy because my father is not good to her. Now you know all about our house. If you wish to go back, I will take you out again."

"Why should I do that?" said Yeshua. "I would rather go on."

Menachem turned his head towards him in the darkness. There was something enigmatic in Yeshua's voice.

"I must warn you," he said, "it is not cheerful." He shoved the tapestry aside and immediately the two of them stood in a luxurious woman's apartment.

A slightly decaying and perfumed impression of flowers and tropical plants, budding and dying simultaneously, prevailed there in the room.

Menachem's mother leaned against the pillows of the couch but her hands refused to lie still. Now they caressed her hair, now her bosom, and now they locked together spasmodically again upon her lap. Menachem ran swiftly to his mother and threw himself on his knees like a young camel.

"Is it you, Menachem? Come to me."

His shoulders fell back, and his mother caught his head in her lap again as though it were a sacrifice.

"Menachem, my comforter," crooned the woman.

"Is there bad news, mother? I heard you weeping."

"Ask rather if there is good news. Does one ask the night whether the heavens are black? Nay, one asks if there are stars in the sky, Menachem. God has closed his doors to our people and myself," the woman groaned again. "What must we do, my son? Go to Jerusalem, go to the rabbis, to Gamaliel who was my father's friend, to Sirach the Hillelite. Perhaps they will teach you what a person must do. Your mother does not know any more. I begged heaven for a child, I, who was barren, I prayed for you but I was already afraid you would be born. I implored you for my sake and already before your birth I feared for your peace. I asked God for a child and I hoped for the child's sake that my wish would be denied. Is there still a man in Israel then who knows which way one must go? A messenger came to tell me that a troop of Roman soldiers seized my brother Azaria near the village of Hebron. They slew him. God knows it is time for Him to fight, isn't that so, Menachem?"

"And father?" asked the boy.

"It goes well with your father. This week he is being welcomed by Antipas in Tiberias and receives a commission" she sighed again. "I have heard it said that your father will not return home alone. He has fallen in love with a young woman. A new wife stands above a forgotten wife, Menachem. New children will come. I fear greatly that your father will forget you completely. The son of Rachel, who is nothing more to him now. It cannot be otherwise. I am growing old."

"It could be otherwise," interrupted Yeshua, who from a distance had taken in the conversation. He was still standing directly in front of the doorway. Behind him on the wall, blue fountains were interwoven in the tapestry.

Menachem knew that it could not be otherwise and he wanted to say so but Yeshua looked handsome in front of the wall curtains and he had spoken without hesitation.

It was only now that his mother saw there was someone else present in her room. She looked up, her eyes fascinated by the figure of the boy, for there was something very detached in Yeshua's demeanor, and yet his body was vigorous as though rooted to the spot where he accidentally stood. The image of a young palm tree flashed instantly through her mind. His eyes wore an expression of strange certainty. The words lay ready in his mouth, his lips parted as though he wished to close them, immediately after he had uttered his words. She had no desire to look at his hair, for she had already seen it.

"Who is this boy?" she asked Menachem.

"He is my friend," answered her son, springing up and standing beside Yeshua. Did he wish to hinder Yeshua from saying he was not Menachem's friend? Was it because Menachem suddenly knew that he and Yeshua formed a pair?

"Come here, boy," said the mother and she gave him a hand, which was not the custom of women in Israel. Yeshua, also against his wont, took her hand.

"I am glad Menachem has a friend," she said. "He has so much to give and to receive! Who are you? But no matter. I've seen you. I know more about you than if I knew your name and origin. I thank you for wanting to be Menachem's friend."

Menachem thought that Yeshua would surely say now: "I am not his friend." For although he was still a child, his sharp powers of discrimination had perceived that for Yeshua uprightness came before compassion. Yet Yeshua remained silent; perhaps he was really Menachem's friend then.

"We are going away now, mother," said Menachem. "We wish to play and talk together. Yeshua is a carpenter's son. His father is Joseph ben Yaacov of Nazareth. He did not want his companions to throw stones at me just because I'm a rich man's son."

"No one is guilty for his birth," remarked Yeshua.

"Nay," said the woman, "no one is responsible for his birth but some people must throw off their birth while others adhere to it firmly. Then if they do no good their guilt begins. But what kind of talk is this for a child? I am a Jerusalemite, Yeshua. And Jerusalem has seen too many things. My father was a pupil of the great Hillel."

"Mother also knows Greek and Latin."

"Oh, I know many languages, too many languages. But what does it avail to know languages in order to read how people slander our folk?"

"In order to bless," said Yeshua.

"In order to bless," repeated the woman. "We always wanted to bless," she continued. "The people take our blessings and give us curses in return. A friend of my father said that a long time ago."

"Still we must bless," insisted Yeshua.

"Yes, still we must bless," agreed the woman, "but it is difficult to bless when they strike us on the hands. You are wise for a boy of your years, Yeshua but I am used to that. Menachem is wise also."

Menachem laid a hand on Yeshua's arm to pull him away from his house which was so mournful but Yeshua took a step closer to the rich woman saying: "Do not weep anymore."

"I shall still have much to lament before I die, isn't that so, Menachem? But when I think of you, Yeshua, I will not cry anymore and I will remember that small stars also shine at night."

Then Yeshua quit the room before Menachem as though he knew the way better.

"The land of Galilee rises in the hills," said a man at the city gates who acted as spokesman for the others. "But we descend the high mountains to Sheol."[1] Menachem thought of these words as he ran down the streets inside the town, seeking the blind alley where Joseph ben Yaacov the carpenter lived.

He found the dwelling of Yeshua's father quickly. A man in grey work clothes stood in front of an open door sawing wood, which projected from a bench. That was surely Joseph.

"Peace be with you!" said Menachem.

"With you also peace!" replied Yeshua's father.

"Where is your son Yeshua?"

Hardly had he spoken when Menachem saw Yeshua standing before him. He did not know whether Yeshua had appeared from a side passage beside the house, from the open doorway or from a street which ran into the carpenter's alley like a small gulley.

"I came to speak to you," said Menachem.

"You came to see our house and to compare it with your own. Afterwards you will say to yourself: "Blessed is Yeshua, for he has it better than I."

1. Hell.

"May I come in?" asked Menachem.

"Surely. All the boys from Nazareth are welcome here."

Menachem stepped into a shabby room which was used for sleeping, cooking and baking.

"Good day, Menachem, peace be with you," said a woman.

He saw a young woman of about twenty-eight, Yeshua's mother.

Yeshua must have spoken of me then, thought the boy.

"Your son is the strongest boy in Nazareth, he saved my life," he said, wanting to please her.

A smile appeared on Miriam's face.

"I have much joy of Yeshua. I am glad when I hear something good of him. Three months before he was born I saw an angel at night. He predicted to me that Yeshua would become a great man in Israel, and he likened me to Sarah and Hannah. It is all very bewildering for a simple woman from Nazareth."

Menachem looked at Yeshua's mother. She had a friendly face.

Over her head she wore a red cloth with yellow ringlets. His eyes surveyed the room. On the east wall which faced Jerusalem somebody had scratched a candlestick in the white plaster. A crude bench stood in a corner. On the long side lay the mats where Yeshua and his parents slept. On a wooden block was a stone beaker which leaked at one end. Into this, oil was poured at night to provide illumination.

"The times are bad," observed Menachem.

Miriam sighed. "The idolators have come again purposely. I heard a man say that with one leap, we . . ."

Menachem was about to retort that violence would only lead Galilee straight to hell but he felt that it did not become him and he did not wish to spoil the good humor of his friend's mother.

"The Romans can do nothing to us!" rang out Yeshua's voice.

"That cannot be said, Yeshua," interrupted Menachem, "they have done us so much evil already. They tortured Ezekiel to death and now they seek his son Yehuda."

"The Romans can only harm us if we permit them!"

And although Menachem was not of the same mind as Yeshua, still he remained silent for he loved the certainty with which his friend spoke.

2

THE DAYS UNDULATED ONCE and forever in their appointed time. The days galloped over time like the horses of mounted legions and never returned. Who sat on the days and rode through time? Only the living and in the midst of these, Yeshua and Menachem. And sometimes the riders met other legions on the backs of days, the events which tore past them. So Yeshua and Menachem rode on the backs of their days. And in the light of the visible days they frequently walked, it chanced, quietly without looking at each other, up the mountainous road to the village of Kefar-Nachum.[1]

Both were now already grown men who were no longer ashamed of their gravity. The times were hard. From Judea to Galilee the fate of Israel reeled from the blows and God's interests suffered. From Judea, where Valerius Gratus oppressed the people and profaned the Invisible Name, came somber tidings. In Galilee men clinched the fist of revolt.

If as Jews they could not live as they wished, they could at least die in their own manner. For they were not afraid of death. The idolators had sucked out the last possession of the Israelites, they had taken away their last earthly joy, but they had also removed their last smoldering vestige of fear and terror.

Yeshua and Menachem brooded over the terrible idolators, while walking, each in his own fashion, and asked themselves fearfully whether a seed of the future still lay in the hard stony ground.

All at once they heard a swelling, buzzing clamor, and a troop of Roman horsemen thundered by. Romans? There were mercenaries there from all the unknown parts of the world—Gauls, Scythians, Germans.

The youths slipped down along the steep slope of the road, under which the valley lay waiting like a loving deathbed. Their fingers clung tightly to the edge of a rock. Their feet found a slight projection in the face of the precipice. If they had not chosen the spot overhanging the abyss, the

---

1. Capernaum.

horsemen would have ridden them underfoot, for the death of the enemy was their business, and the death of the innocent their diversion.

"I want to see what they are up to," whispered Menachem. "They are taking the road to Nazareth. Let's climb up the path and follow them."

"Nay," said Yeshua. "I have naught to do with idolators."

Menachem pressed his feet against the precipice, braced his knees and elbows and stood up on the road again. He had a light step and great endurance. He ran after the troop of horsemen but by now the riders were hidden from view by a wagon and its driver. Menachem trotted still harder and shot over the road like a leopard. One jump and he grabbed the high back wall of the wagon firmly while letting his feet trail over the wheels.

"If the driver sees he has a traveler, I will grab him by the shoulders and strangle him. I will slay him like Moses slew the Egyptian."

The soldiers were commanded by an officer with the high overbearing type of Roman face. They rode into the town of Nazareth where the command "Halt!" resounded. When the men sprang from their horses Menachem slid under the wagon. The commander assigned some soldiers to find shelter for the animals; three of them took the reins and immediately marched away.

Menachem crawled to the back of the wagon, stole to the edge of the road and slowly stood erect. He was just about to step out as an ordinary pedestrian when the captain espied him and ordered one of his men to bring him the young Jew.

"Galilean?"

"Nay, Judean."

"Do you live here?"

"Aye."

"Are there many strong youths in his place?"

"Nay, Nazareth is poor. The men have gone away. The authorities have taken away the farmers" ploughs and confiscated the tools of the tradesmen. They cannot earn a living here anymore. Therefore they have gone to Tiberias and Caesarea where money can be found."

"We can use you, boy. We have need of men—for the slave mart. They ought to bring the money you have hidden from Caesar's treasury. Show me and my men the way. If we catch ten of them we will set you free and your father will not need to redeem you from slavery. Now show us the way."

At that instant Menachem uttered a piercing scream and struck the Roman commander's chin with his skull. The soldiers set out in pursuit but Menachem had already disappeared in the running maze of streets which were traversed by small blind alleys where it was impossible to tell one house from another in the public road—unless the idolators set fire to the buildings.

In those days all the people of Nazareth knew the Jerusalemite and looked upon him as a familiar stranger in their midst. As a child he had been a dreamer, a refined son of the capital. Who knew what he had in his mind? As a young man he made it a point of honor to be a helper to the townspeople of Nazareth, a simple friend of everyone in the village, one who enters everywhere and to whom each one said: "Shalom Aleichem."[2]

He helped the women carry water or thresh grain and an old man to chop wood. Why he did this he did not know. Probably out of compassion. Menachem was like a tree which must stretch its branches downward in order to protect something from rotting and falling asunder.

Despite his gauntness the Jerusalemite had developed into a handsome youth. Even in this land of black-haired people, the glint of his smooth, luxurious hair was striking. His swift gliding movements, his almost dancing gait had a certain charm. Precisely because Menachem loved the daily life of the earth was he noticed by all the young women and maidens of Nazareth. He was thinking of one of them, of Yocheved, the daughter of Abba ben Alexander when he fled from the Romans. Her house was a large one in front of the village and he knew of a hole in the ground there through which he could enter. The Romans, most likely, would not search for him there, for old Abba—who was somewhat domineering—possessed no sons.

Thus Menachem raced up the streets southwards from which Mount Tabor now appeared, now vanished in the panorama. Finally he reached a road of which only one side was occupied by houses. From this road a small footpath branched out. Menachem sped around the corner of the path and disappeared through a hole in the ground.

God would not permit His people to fall apart and be scattered individually. Life had to be communal for events affected the whole community. So once again there was public mourning, this time over the little town of Nazareth.

---

2. "Peace be upon you"—a standard Israelite greeting.

Only the week before the inhabitants had refused a tribute which the Tetrarch Antipas had proclaimed in the name of the Romans. There was nothing more to be found in Nazareth so they had sent word to the Idumean. Nothing but bitter pain. Cut us in two, you will find nothing!

And now Rome had arrived on a man-hunt for its money. Within three quarters of an hour the town changed its aspect three times. It was normal when Menachem's shrieks gave a voice to one specific meaning. Then all life was sucked from the streets and it became a dead city. The strangers battered down the doors, windows and walls with axes, pickaxes, clubs and stones. The contents of the houses spilled onto the streets. They set fire to the rat holes and drove the rodents outside. These, however, were people. When would man understand that people were human beings, not animals. God had never said to mankind in the book of Genesis: "I give your fellow man into your hands. Use him. Enjoy him."

That was the question on Yeshua's mind as he beheld the acts of violence. He feared not for himself nor did he offer relief, as it was still for him to decide whether he would choose to feed on wormwood and bitter herbs.

In times of great anguish the holiest people and whatever they hold most sacred are sacrificed in the marketplace. Where others are present, and precisely because others are present, they give up their attachment to a child, a man, a sweetheart, to life itself, on the communal altar.

The soldiers searched the houses and hovels, dragging away men and youths to which the women clung tenaciously like dogs that refuse to release the meat which must nourish them.

"Nazareth is descending into Sheol!" wailed the man who dispensed wisdom at the city gate. It was a bright, clear day in the month of Sivan but grief and weeping filled the streets of Nazareth and screams rent the air like yellow lightning.

Yeshua wondered what he would do if the Romans dragged away his father, a man of fifty. Surely Miriam his mother would cling to him tightly and refuse to let him go. Perhaps a idolator would kick her in the stomach then.

At that moment Yehudith, wife of the tinsmith, clung frantically to her husband while two Romans dragged him away by chains around the wrist. They had probably found the chains in his workshop. The tinsmith was thirty years old and the father of three children.

Where would he die now? As an eunuch in Alexandria? Withered by the sun in the land of Kush? Had he begotten three children for this? Was it for this that his parents had looked at him gratefully when he was born? "Why must this be?" asked Yeshua. And still the events glided past him like time through space.

If they dragged away his father, Miriam would also cling tightly to Joseph. That too, Yeshua would have to witness in grief. He would have to sacrifice and give up so much before he could intervene.

How should a person intervene?

Close beside he heard an old man's voice crying: "Yeshua, Yeshua, flee. They are coming. They are abducting young men!" But Yeshua did not flee. The old sandal maker Amitai who had warned him to flee was running to meet the Romans himself. Two huge blond men from the lands beyond the sea had seized his son. They kicked his son in the shins for he struggled to break free. Then did Amitai make a ridiculous jump for such an old man and flung his arms around the neck of his tall son. He pressed his shriveled body against him as though they were a lover and his mistress.

"My son, my only son!"

The foreign soldiers remained motionless for the boy was almost falling. A Roman centurion approached and said in broken Aramaic:

"Stop your yapping or we slay your son. Away, hop!"

They tore the old man away from his son. Amitai could not stand the shock and toppled lengthwise to the ground like a beast hurled through space. In an instant he realized what had happened. Two worlds had locked into one another like cogs. The old man raised his hands and murmured to the Romans in a language they did not understand:

"By what right do you take away my son, idolators? Even Israel has no right to drag him away for no one shall deprive an old father of his only child and breadwinner."

"What is he mumbling?" demanded the commander. "Forward."

Suddenly the soldiers who held Amitai's son fast felt a stabbing pain behind their loins. Collapsing, they loosed the chains. Amitai's son was free again.

"After him!" roared the commander. Side by side with another who had loomed up behind him, the son of the sandal maker raced up the road.

"Damned nuisance! Now cast the old man down the mountain."

Three mercenaries trampled Amitai underfoot. They stuck the points of their sandals under his ribs. So they set him rolling until he reached the edge of the road where he tried to raise himself. A soldier hurled the half-raised figure back to the ground. He tried to grasp hold of a couple of stones with his brittle aged fingers, willing to pierce the palms of his hands with their sharp projections in order to remain hanging. The idolaters diverted themselves with his despair. Six feet gave him a savage kick over the length of his cringing body. Inevitably the moment came. The force of gravity prevailed and his soul let go. Screaming, Amitai rolled ever faster down the steep slope into the crevice below where his body was shattered like a pitcher.

Numbed by the spectacle, Yeshua continued leaning against the wall.

"Is this man? Why do I not intervene and lay hands upon these Romans? I would gladly interfere even if the idolaters kill me. How sweet is death when one has seen this. 'How fair are thy tents, oh Jacob; how beautiful thy cities, oh Israel.' Does that mean the dwellings of the dead, perhaps?"

But Yeshua might not die yet, therefore he went homewards. By some miraculous agency the Romans had not seen him. Menachem's arrival too had escaped their notice. Menachem had loomed up abruptly behind Amitai's son, had saved Barzilai and indirectly caused the death of Amitai.

"Maybe it means that I must count on Menachem," mused Yeshua. "The one may pursue the path which he must follow because another has been sent out upon the road to balance the scale."

Like a fox Menachem slipped through the hole under the wall of Abba Alexander's house. He crept a short distance through a narrow underground tunnel. The tunnel turned lighter and a window appeared in the hollow opening. Having emerged, Menachem made haste across an empty patch of ground to a gate through which he entered an inner garden. Here one could stroll endlessly around a luxurious center fountain.

His friend Yocheved welcomed him. The young maiden thought often of Menachem. Whenever she heard noises upon the road she hoped it would be him. This time the noise had not deceived her.

"Is it you, Menachem?"

"I sought shelter, Yocheved. The idolaters are all over Nazareth. They are taking away the men to sell them as slaves. Where is your mother?"

"Come into the house, I'll hide you."

"I shall not stay long, Yocheved."

"Are you afraid for me? Do you wish to have nothing to thank me for?"

"Nay, it is not that! I do not wish to stray far from the street and the people."

"Live more for yourself Menachem, so you can also live for another. You don't understand the ways in which a person can be in need, Menachem."

"Our whole village, our whole people are in dire need."

"You have no compassion for the anguish that one soul can experience, Menachem. Have you ever held me in your thoughts?"

"Immerse your soul in the grief of your people, Yocheved. I hold not with a grief that differs from the grief of my neighbor."

"I understand you not," Menachem. "Are you glad that I am near you?"

"I am overjoyed to see you. Your beauty does me good and I take delight in your beautiful voice. Our maidens are like flowers withered by the dust of the roads. Only some of them receive water."

"Come with me, I shall hide you."

"And what if your father and mother perceive that you are concealing a young man?"

"My father and mother never perceive anything. Like me, they are too busy with themselves."

Menachem followed Yocheved on tiptoe into the house. They entered a long, narrow side gallery and came to a halt before a closed door. Moans issued from the room beyond.

"That is my mother," said Yocheved. "Listen to her lamentations."

"Where is he? Where is he?" the mother's voice called out. "Perhaps they have carried him off and I may never find him again!"

"She is speaking of her guilty love," whispered Yocheved. "She has a lover!"

They walked further through the house of Abba Alexander until they reached a curtained door on the ground floor. Men's voices resounded from the inside. They seemed to be having a debate.

"That is my father," said Yocheved. "He is discussing a problem of Halacha[3] with Chanan ben Yosai his friend."

"He studies while the Romans hunt the men of Nazareth?" asked Menachem.

"He always studies, he studies perversely, straight through the grief of his daughter because no young man will take her away."

"Because my road leads far astray."

"I know it. But say no more. He studies straight through the adultery and grief of his wife; he studies in spite of God himself! He takes everything

3. Jewish law; the way of life according to the rabbinic commentaries.

true upon the road and still he sees nothing. Father is a true Pharisee, Menachem."

"I understand him. Without the Law he is cold but why does he study the Law precisely now while the Romans are removing our men? I cannot stay here, Yocheved. I will not hide anymore. I will return to the street."

"Stay, Menachem, the Romans will carry you off."

But he loosened his arm from her grip.

"Remain, Menachem, they will take you away from me . . . they will torture you, Menachem my only friend."

But Menachem no longer heard her. He was back on the open terrain, returning to the road. He was protected by the same mysterious power which watched over Yeshua. He traversed the town of Nazareth by the outside roads which led inward to the heart of the marketplace. The streets were full of struggling people. Screaming women raised their naked arms to the sky. Some cursed the Romans, their mouths frozen in a right angular breach. The howls of the children, the song of helplessness testified to the violence of the strangers like a mournful choir.

Everywhere Menachem saw interlaced people. They struck and injured each other while their puny arms and hands clung frantically to those who were being dragged away. But hands cannot hold the souls of those who are being torn from each other nor reverse the events that tear them asunder.

Simple people in whose huts Menachem had stayed, with whom he had spoken at night in front of the door, became outlaws.

Menachem saw how the strong young smith was taken away; he heard the piercing scream of his wife Yehudith as she dragged her cluster of babies behind her. He saw how they led away Amitai's son. A little old woman who screamed that her grandchild was lost received a blow on the head, fell down and was trampled by a rolling wave of struggling people.

Thou shalt not murder! said the Law. But there were exceptions in this miserable life. One might not kill unless he saw evil men slaying innocent people. Menachem firmly gripped the dagger which he wore in his girdle under his cloak. Old Amitai had leaped like a monkey to the warm breast of his son and the Roman dogs had torn him away from the youth.

Menachem sneaked behind the soldiers. He stabbed them in the back one after the other. Together with Amitai's son Barzilai he hurried down the road to escape the Romans.

The two young men did not remain together for long. Menachem darted into the smelly alley of the tanners. Leaping like a goat, he was racing across the dirt of the steeply rising alley when he heard a woman's voice screaming from a low roof.

"They used me! Better mud in my house than their seed. Be you from Israel, man? Then catch!" A woman flung down a bundle which he caught. As Menachem ran he noticed that he was bearing a child in his arms.

3

IT WAS NIGHT OVER Nazareth. Where the highway curved into the Great Sea, the men that escaped the Roman marauders had called a rendezvous.

"Judgment has been cast," said a man who expected a stark descent into Sheol. "God has sent His tempest. We must bow to its waves and billows. We find ourselves on board the shipwreck of the Lord." Others gnashed their teeth with rage and despair as the prophets had foretold.

A full moon shone peacefully and solemnly over the men. The night wind moaned through the mountains. At the head of the large assembly stood the fully grown Yeshua, his eyes filled with compassion. His squarely trimmed beard was chestnut brown and black like his hair. The great smith Shammai towered over them like a giant, his hand gripping the handle of his hammer with its head on the ground. Among them were the young shepherd Pinchas with his curly black hair around a bronzed scalp and the itinerant merchant Andreas Philippos. Shirach the potter who had succumbed to despair strolled about aimlessly, hoping that others would give them clear instructions on what to do.

"We cannot stay and look on," shouted the smith. "We are here because we have hidden ourselves like fugitive slaves. Slaves we were in Egypt but free men in our own land. Must we also become slaves in our own country? We are going away, men, we choose the mountains. There can be no more rest for the men of Israel. In Judea they are fighting already. Yehuda the Galilean has assembled thousands of men. They lie in wait for the idolators. Every act of resistance is a spade of earth for the place where God digs Rome's grave. It is written: blood for blood. I have seen enough blood since the time my father showed me the first idolator."

"Tonight I bade my wife goodbye and made her understand that from now on she must consider herself a widow. My children are orphans. Will any among you go with me? Early tomorrow morning parents will look in vain for their children and women will grope for a shadow. Otherwise are we all guilty!"

"And what say you, Yeshua?" asked Pinchas the shepherd.

Yeshua looked at him long and piercingly. Then he answered:

"The time is not yet come."

Shammai the smith raised the hammer block gently from the ground and let it fall again.

"The time has come."

"For you but not for me," replied Yeshua tautly.

"And what is your counsel, Menachem? You are young but you share what stirs in us," said Andreas Philippos.

They did not know whether Menachem had just joined the group from the darkness or whether he had been standing there a long time already. He was slimmer than ever, the young Judean, but tenacious and wiry.

"I know that Yeshua speaks with God. But each one is free and may switch his path at any moment. Woe be to man and woe be to people that each hour of their life is marked upon the crossroads. Where there is choice, there is darkness."

"Where there is choice, there is darkness," repeated Yeshua, adopting Menachem's words for the first time.

"For us there is no choice!" cried Shammai the smith. "Today we saw our children dragged away as slaves. I have seen my son for the last time. There is no choice."

"If there is no choice for you, then go," said Menachem. "Then has your hour come."

Yeshua stood motionless at the edge of the group. Looking at him, the others did not know whether he was sunk in thought or whether his mind was, in truth, somewhere else.

A night wind rustled softly behind the group of hopeless men.

"We give everything up, we are going," called the shepherd, the merchant, the young wood chopper, the pottery bakers, the sons of the donkey driver. "We follow the smith."

Menachem looked at them with compassion. But Yeshua continued to stand there as before with impassive eyes—as though this event was not of this world.

Led by the smith, the men moved off to the south towards the wild hills of Judea.

"Where to, Yeshua?" asked Menachem.

"Where my Father wills there will I go," replied Menachem, abruptly taking over the words of his friend. For he understood that Yeshua meant God.

"Does a Father wish then that one son should go here and another one yonder?" asked Yeshua.

"Aye, Yeshua, for the sake of their Mother's house."

Yeshua gazed at Menachem under the still moon which hung over the mountain like a glass bell and although their eyes were compassionate and earnest too, they could not subdue one another.

Silently Yeshua turned around to take the road to Nazareth while Menachem cautiously descended the mountain slope towards a forest which rose up from the stony ground like the plume of some subterranean creature. There he lay down in order to reflect on what to do the following day.

Menachem fell into a heavy sleep in which he did not dream but when dawn approached it seemed that he saw sunlight and wished to get up but could not as he lay under a lump of rock. He tried to roll over in order to dislodge the stone. He bent his arm to the elbow, exerting all his strength to heave the boulder; it was no use.

Then he opened his eyes, sighed deeply and realized that the dream was part of this world. For a man pressed his knee on Menachem's chest and his hands pushed Menachem's shoulders to the ground.

"Who are you?" asked the man.

"A witness of my people!"

"Are you also a witness of your people?"

"Aye!"

"Who are your people?"

"I am a Hebrew!"

"So—you know the prophets! Do you serve God or the idolators?"

"I know not whom I serve. I wish to serve my own people but not against God."

"Your name?"

"Oppressed people have no name!"

"You are right." With a spring the man leaped up and Menachem recovered the freedom of his chest and arms.

"Now—your name?"

"Menachem, son of Gedalia who calls himself Marcus Mercator. Now what is your name?"

"They call me Ben Nesher."

"What, the son of the eagle? I have heard of you. You belong to the partisans of Yehuda the Galilean."

"That is so. The idolators follow closely on my heel. I seek shelter for a day or two. Hide me. But you are free. If you will not hide me I will not slay you. If you betray me, however, then it is all over with the house of Marcus Mercator."

"Let us go," said Menachem.

So the two young men walked together in the direction of Nazareth, not along the main road but through a path formed by nature which crossed the slope irregularly, at intervals broken or hidden by palm groves. Now and then their steps flushed out some mountain badgers that despite their plumpness scattered swiftly before their feet. Perhaps they had prepared the path that Menachem and Ben Nesher followed.

This Ben Nesher was a great and fearful name in Israel. He was an avenger of God who had sworn never to rest until the Romans were driven from the holy soil. Woe to the Israelite who was unwilling to place his goods, chattel and livestock in the service of God and Israel. Ben Nesher was tall of stature, broad and gaunt, flat like an iron slab on which houses might be built. People who were as broad-shouldered as Ben Nesher were seldom so lean. His hair was black, unruly and bent in curls like claws upon his skull. His face was regular, his nose hooked and his chin protruding and hard like a buffer block. Justly was a man with such outward appearance called Son of the Eagle.

"Life in Judea is hard, is it not?" said Menachem.

"One rests softer on the hills there than in the beds of Jerusalem," answered Ben Nesher, measuring Menachem with his eye.

"You belong to the runners. You have long strong fingers! Do you still sleep in your bed, do you wait at home each morning for the arrival of the tax collector? Do you wish to pay the great idolator in Rome so that you may live, and give him what you owe to God? Are you a Galilean?"

"Nay, I live in Nazareth but I am from Judea."

"The men of Judea live best in the hills of Judea."

"Do you believe it will last long, Ben Nesher?"

"What? The rule of the idolators? I know not. I am no prophet and no Essene. I have no future to predict. Today I must fight the idolators. The book of Daniel says that the end of the fourth kingdom of the fourth enemy of God will surely come. We shall not live so far. He who does not shun death, serves God. To him nothing can happen and he does his duty."

"Is there a future for Israel, Ben Nesher?"

"That is for God to decide but we must change the present."

"Should we not husband our strength then for the age to come?"

"He who spares himself commits treason. People who should have died and who perish not in battle are false coins; they have been usurers in their duty!"

Menachem remained silent a long time and Ben Nesher did not feel compelled to speak. Life among the stones had made him taciturn.

Does this man see nothing but his own vision? wondered Menachem. The field in which it grew was once tilled and irrigated. He does not yet know from which feeling his idea was born? In his head he has a nut with a hard shell but he cannot find the soil, the roots and the tree again. He turns the nut around and around. Perhaps it must be so. Perhaps one should be cut off from one's feelings as soon as the feeling has given birth. Ben Nesher walked another way than Yeshua. Surely, the people stood at a crossroads.

And God Himself? Did he like to stand at a crossroads too? Or had God intended this for His chosen people? It hurts to stand at a crossroads forever but if that is Israel's destiny, may a child of Israel desire a better fate than the people?

Then Menachem said: "I have thought this over, Ben Nesher. I shall conceal you and accompany you for a while afterwards."

The dawn began to glow, caressing the distant valley and mountains of Hermon that dominated the northern horizon. A flock of cranes flew over the plain of Esdrelon. Other large birds, the pelicans from the Sea of Kinnereth, also crossed the sky.

"I know a place where you will be safe, Ben Nesher! The Romans will not seek you there!"

They reached a spot on the slope where a stair had been carved. Ascending the crude steps, they arrived at a steeply rising path protected by rocky walls on both sides. The path led to a narrow alley, a miserable little street where dogs sniffed the heaps of garbage outside the houses. The white of the walls was sulfur-yellow, stained with dingy black spots. Garbage water trickled over the stones that served as a natural pavement. At the corner of this street in a gulley called the Alley of the Jackals—these animals sometimes penetrated there at night—they reached the house of Joseph the carpenter. A wooden fence enclosing a workshop extended from the dwelling. A door had been built in the fence.

Work was already beginning in the house of the carpenter. In front of the door stood Joseph behind his bench. He did not notice the two young men approaching. In the middle of the alley they saw Yeshua standing with his arms folded across his chest. It was as though he had been awaiting them.

"Yeshua," said Menachem, "here is Ben Nesher, the friend of Yehuda the Galilean. He seeks shelter for a day or two. Inside this enclosure is a dry hole, I know. May Ben Nesher stay here?"

Yeshua stood there as ever in his own immobility which made others, even old people, uneasy because that quiescence seemed to contain all movement. It was the immobility of momentarily folded wings. He looked at Menachem and then at Ben Nesher. The latter did not lower his eyes but was stirred by Yeshua and, turning to Menachem, said:

"Now there's a man! Is he coming over to us?"

"I think not," said Menachem. "We all have different paths. There are too many roads for our people."

"There is only one way for man," interrupted Yeshua.

"There is also only one way for our people," said Ben Nesher. "God and our freedom!"

Menachem wished to bring this conversation to an end so he asked again:

"Yeshua, may Ben Nesher stay here?"

And now a singular thing happened. Menachem had followed Yeshua from his fourteenth to his nineteenth year but had never seen him laugh.

Now the young man smiled. His smile had a strange effect on Menachem; it was as though he had just witnessed an unusual phenomenon of nature.

"In my Father's house there is place for all," said Yeshua.

Menachem nodded; Yeshua had spoken of his Father's house for the second time.

"Yeshua knows what his Father wills, Ben Nesher! Go in!" Menachem opened the door in the fence.

Ben Nesher looked at both young men. "You have helped me. That is still not one tenth of the work. You may depend upon it that I will not leave here alone. He who is not with us is unclean."

"So also says Yochanan the Baptist who washes away sins in the Jordan," observed Menachem. "There is too much talking in Israel. Each one has his own surety. But where is the real certainty when there are so many?"

"In faith," replied Yeshua.

"There are too many beliefs, people must be careful. Each heart has its own niche," remarked Menachem.

Yeshua turned away from them and Menachem shrugged his shoulders in a melancholy way. Yet Yeshua turned back, walked over to Ben Nesher—who had made himself a nest between the boards of a low shed—to tell him that he would bring him some blankets.

4

MENACHEM RETURNED TO HIS mother's house no more for he knew that only a few servants and his father's agent had remained behind. His father travelled much and Menachem feared that he did good business with the Tetrarch of Galilee, the sly fox Herod Antipas.

Marcus Mercator had taken a new wife unto himself, the daughter of a Greek Jew and an Edomite, and found joy therein. His father lived with the times, he had left those who grieve and proved in advance that one can escape the affliction of one's people, albeit only for a time. His mother had returned to Jerusalem out of longing for the world of her childhood.

Absorbed in thoughts of Ben Nesher and his destiny, he headed in the direction of the Sea of Kinnereth, Then he turned back to Nazareth in order to meet Ben Nesher whom he had resolved to accompany. The Romans offended Israel greatly. The time for prudence had passed. In the book of Koheleth[1] it was recommended how one ought to divide one's time. Menachem remembered the line "There is a time for saving and a time for giving."

Satisfied with his decision, Menachem re-ascended the street of the carpenters until he reached the alley of the jackals. He entered the enclosure and looked in the dry shed. Ben Nesher has vanished. And now there came a strange feeling over Menachem, for not only was Ben Nesher gone, but he likewise missed Yeshua's presence. He ran into the house. In the only room which served as their dwelling sat Joseph the carpenter with his head in his hands. Miriam stood before the fire with tear-stained eyes.

"Where is Ben Nesher, the captain of Yehuda the Galilean?"

Joseph raised his arms and let them fall again.

Menachem looked around the low room. Never had he seen an enclosed space so empty or barren.

1. Ecclesiastes.

"He is gone," replied Joseph and Miriam at the same time in an anxious tone.

"With Ben Nesher?"

"Are there still parallel roads then in Israel?" asked Miriam with a sob in her throat.

"Nay, not with Ben Nesher," replied Joseph.

"He could not be otherwise," groaned Miriam, and Joseph agreed with a sigh: "He could not be otherwise."

"But it falls heavy on us. Yeshua was our light," said Miriam.

"Let's go outside, mother," suggested Menachem. "It is too dark in here."

Miriam understood Menachem; she bent under the low door and sat down on a bench in front of the hut. The young man sat down beside her, reaching out his hand which Miriam took and held in her lap while softly muttering: "Ben ami" which means "son of my people."

Then she began to speak in a mournful voice. "He could not be otherwise but why not?" We know not why he has quit his father's house without saying goodbye to us and waiting for our blessing."

"It must have been hard for him also, Miriam."

"It is hard for him but God knows where he must go. He was our light. Why did it have to be extinguished now?"

Then Miriam fell into the lamentations and recollections of a mother who stores the daily life of her child in the treasure-house of her soul. For a mother is nourished by her weaned children.

"Yeshua was ever a strange child, Menachem. Perhaps that was bound up with the dream I had when I carried him. Once many years ago his father and I went with him to Jerusalem to celebrate the Passover feast. There were many with us from Nazareth and surrounds. We celebrated the festival joyously, ate the matzos in the field outside the city and each day we went together to the Beit HaMikdash."[2]

"During the first days of the festival I never saw Yeshua happier than in the Temple. He looked around all over as though he wanted to carry everything away with him. But toward the end of the festival he said: 'I will not return there for the present.'"

"'Why?' his father and I asked.

'Because I can see nothing in front of me but the ground and I wish to look up.' Thus the last days he did not go with us to the Holy Temple."

2. The House of Holiness, the Temple.

"Then came the time when the festival was over and we began to count the summer days. Our people from Nazareth went back with other groups from the neighborhood and we remained together. For we had to pass through the land of Samaria. After the Passover feast the Samaritans are not to be trusted because they are jealous of the Temple in Jerusalem.

Yeshua walked with us and from time to time I set him on top of Sirach the farmer's donkey. The second morning I wished to comb his hair. He was gone. And he had not slept beside me that night. His father and I were greatly disturbed. We ran from one group to the other.

But Yeshua was not there and no one had seen him. Should we mourn over him? I could not do it. I prayed to God: 'Take my life. But let me not mourn over Yeshua and let me not live if my child does not live. You spared Isaac for the sake of Sarah and Samuel for the sake of Hannah. You have not taken him away, that cannot be.' Then I found peace. A whole morning I had peace but his father still wandered around seeking him with eyes cast down. At midday I became uneasy again. One's confidence does not last long when something dear to you is lost. It is a sin; one should have faith but so much had happened. At midday I became sorely uneasy once more so I sought him in the multitudes again. God heard me calling and imploring 'Yeshua, Yeshua, my child!'

He did not come. Had the bears caught him? I covered my eyes with my hands. Could it be that the Samaritans had carried him off for service on top of Mount Gerizim because he was a Jew?

'We may not mourn yet, wife,' said my husband.

'We may not mourn yet,' I said to him.

Then God gave me peace. We went on. We gave ourselves additional respite. And when we arrived in Nazareth, the child stood at the door. I fell upon the ground and I called out: 'Blessed be God. Praised be the Lord, for He gives children to a mother and He does not take them away before He has taken the mother!'"

"Amen!" said Joseph. "May His Name be praised forever and ever."

"But Yeshua did not understand; he stared at us with eyes wide. He only asked: 'Why were you afraid?'"

"Later we heard that he had been with some pious learned men and had talked to them like a wise man from Jerusalem."

Then Miriam began to weep. "But now he has gone away and I know not whither. Then he was nine years old. Now he is twenty. I cannot be with him anymore."

"God is with him," said Menachem.

"I cannot be with him anymore," said Miriam sadly. "God keeps a reckoning with a man of twenty years but not with his mother."

"Yeshua believes that a man should have faith," declared Menachem, although he knew that Yeshua meant a type of faith that did not exclude the dead. "Yeshua has useful work to do, he will return. You will see him walking on the roads of Galilee with friends who hearken to him eagerly. Yeshua is not like other children, Miriam."

"I know it, I know it," sighed his mother. "He is a strange person. That I already heard when I still had to give birth to him. Unusual children weigh heaviest in the arms and heart of a mother. Heaviest and warmest. When they leave, the concern and the fear become worse."

"It is so," said Menachem, "but I think of Yeshua. He drives and dedicates himself ever harder. I must go now, Miriam. I shall seek him for you."

"Why are you so good to me, Menachem?"

"Because Yeshua is my friend."

"But he has spoken little of you to me."

"Yeshua speaks little. Yet he is my friend."

"Is there no other reason, Menachem?"

"Because the mothers in Israel weigh heavy upon my heart, Miriam."

"Comforter!"

"Perhaps, of those who remain behind! I will return on the festival to see you again, and to speak with you more about Yeshua."

She took his hand and said again: "Ben ami!"

"Bath ami" he whispered, which means "daughter of my people."

For in Menachem a calling was growing to be a friend of his people.

Afterwards Menachem went to seek Ben Nesher. He could not understand why the patriot had left earlier than the time they had agreed upon.

Menachem knew Lower Galilee like the back of his hand. He wandered along the paths that trailed over the hills, he searched in forests and behind the trunks of cedars. He watched all the roads which led out from Nazareth but he found Ben Nesher nowhere. The few trusted ones whom he could question about the captain did not even know he had been in the area. What to do now? Go north to the Syrian border where the threatening Hermon rose up like a misty giant? To the east where the Roman servant in Tiberias availed himself of the corrupt times to fill his pockets? To the sea where the comfortable Roman rests his legs on Israel's gaunt belly? Or to the south? He surmised that Ben Nesher had set out for the mountains of Judea where rebels had in the past felt safest. Thus he decided to quit his beloved Nazareth with the people he knew and the fertile bed of Galilee under its blankets of grass and crops. He would go to austere Judea which God had designed Himself and there seek Ben Nesher. For he wore the rebel leader's brand and chain until another encounter would bring another instruction.

But first Menachem turned back to Nazareth to bid his friend Yocheved farewell. He entered the front door of the house of the Pharisee Abba Alexander and headed straight to the rooms where he expected Yocheved to be. The apartments through which he passed were dark. Suddenly he felt two arms holding him captive.

"Is it you, Menachem?"

"Aye. I come to take farewell of you for the present and to see the child. Then I go to Judea. My mother awaits me."

"It is not true, Menachem. You are going into danger. You are afraid that you are neglecting your duty. Speak softly. There is danger here. A stranger has pushed himself into the house. I fear for the life of my father. Feel this and follow me."

Menachem touched Yocheved's hands. They were gripping a sharp object.

She took his hands and said: "Follow me."

They came to the room of Abba Alexander and overheard a heated dispute.

"Two thousand drachmas, not a coin less!"

"I repeat it, man. I cannot give it to you and I won't!"

"So, old miser, you have nothing left for your people then? My men and I sleep on the rocks, eat locusts, can be captured and slain by the idolators at any moment, and you refuse the small relief with which we must buy food and weapons?"

"And how do I know you do not extort the gold for yourself?"

"If you had eyes in your head, you would be able to discern that."

"I will not give it."

"I must have it, otherwise . . ."

"I won't give it!"

"You do not wish to help your people then?"

"I do not wish to plunge my people into misfortune!"

"There you have now the Pharisees. Fine detached people. They study the Law day and night but God's honor is not worth two thousand drachmas."

"You are exposing us to danger."

"We wish to purify the land. It is impossible to wear the yoke of the Romans and serve God at the same time."

"For him who follows the Law nothing is impossible, young man. If you wish to be true to God's Law you can live everywhere, and if that is not possible, die everywhere. There is no other way."

"Only two thousand drachmas!"

"There is no other way. Life outside the Law is a shadow, it is separation from the substance. But you think only of life outside the mitzvoth.[3] You speak of God's Honor and you mean your vanity!"

"Hand over, man. He who permits himself to be defiled by the Romans on the outside, reflects it on the inside. I demand two thousand drachmas."

"You think I'm a miser. I shall give to the Temple."

"The Temple receives enough. I demand two thousand drachmas, otherwise . . ."

"Otherwise, what?"

"Your house goes up in flames and for you I have something too!"

Yocheved tried to shove the curtain aside but Menachem forestalled her gesture. The man who wished to wound Abba Alexander stood now with his back to them so Yocheved could have stabbed him. Menachem who had recognized the voice of the stranger pushed Yocheved back and entered the Pharisee's room first.

"Abba, I know this man. He is Ben Nesher, the captain of Yehuda the Galilean. Give him the two thousand drachmas which he demands."

"And who gives you the right, young man, to tell me what I must do?"

"Because Ben Nesher is too good for you to make him a sinner. It is written, 'Thou shalt not murder!'"

"I will not give the money because I may not give it. They wish to know better than God and to act ahead of God. The end has not yet come. They want to bring it closer by violence against God's purpose."

"We only know what we must do, Abba. That is the only thing we know of God's design. Hand over the money."

"Nay."

"Then I let Ben Nesher do his work. I crave your forgiveness, Yocheved."

3. Righteous deeds.

"Will you let my father be murdered, Menachem?"

"I shall not lift my hand against anyone who has sacrificed his blood for Israel."

There followed a few moments of silence. Then Abba Alexander arose.

"Good, the wise men say that when one is threatened by danger he may break the Law, except when the oppressor demands that God's Holy name be defiled. I shall give up the gold to buy my life. At this moment I eat unclean flesh. I shall atone for this."

Abba Alexander opened a closet where he stored his money chest. He counted out the gold to the captain.

"I do not love my father. There is no tenderness in him," said Yocheved softly to Menachem. "I hold not with his interpretation. But when you refused to fight for him I loved him."

"I go to fight for Ben Nesher. He loves us so much that he has become our despair."

"Have you nothing left over for me then, Menachem? Will you not take one step out of your way for me? Do I mean so little to you that you cannot do for me nor leave me one deed, that you cannot postpone one intention for my sake?"

"You counsel me ill, Yocheved."

"In you too, there is no tenderness, Menachem. There is no more tenderness among the men of this folk."

"My tenderness will come when you no longer put yourself first, Yocheved. God keep and protect you!"

"Colder than ice are the words of a man whom one loves in vain. God be with you, Menachem."

Then the young man gripped the great Ben Nesher by the arm. "I was coming to seek you and did not think I would find you so close. I am going with you."

With swift steps the two men abandoned the house of Yocheved, who stood near a window staring after them:

"My lover deserts my house like a thief. Now I remain behind with a father who lives not among humans. He does not even notice me. The least of the commentaries in the Mi-Sinai[4] which his wise men say is derived from the Law of Sinai, is dearer to him than my soul. One cannot serve God and people at the same time, no matter what they say. My mother has

4. Oral law.

run off with her lover. This is no house in which to stay. Its doors are shut but in all of Nazareth there is no house more open and colder. I shall run away also. May not a chaste virgin do the same as an adulterous wife—run after a man?"

5

"ALTHOUGH YOU ARE CONFUSED I shall take you with me," said Ben Nesher during the first quarter of the moon as they descended the road together to cross the land of Samaria to the south.

"You balance and weigh and reflect too much, and you wish to respect Abraham and Marcus and Alexander and Hanina and Simon and Reuben and the majesty of the sun and the mournful time of the moon. Hark you, that won't do. A man can only take one responsibility upon himself. Seek out some great cause. I have chosen Israel. Still I shall take you with me since you are eager. They say that bloodshed makes a man insatiable. Much blood must flow over your hands before you properly love that which you fight for. Blood clings, Menachem. It clings firmly to whatever you love."

"I am no Pharisee," said Menachem, "and no Sadducee or Essene as I know that if you obey God too much on one side, you disobey him on the other. Why is it written that you shall not murder? You have almost forgotten it. You murder too easily. I go with you and I shall tell you why. He who will not build each day for fear he possesses not the perfect plan for the house of the future, his children will surely have no roof over their heads."

Ben Nesher and Menachem did not remain alone. From all sides, from caves along the hidden paths of the mountains emerged men who joined them in the long journey from Nazareth to Judea, expected and unexpected, acquaintances and strangers. They followed Ben Nesher and Menachem like wolves behind sheep. They dropped like birds of prey from the mountain tops into the growing troop.

So they came to Sichem and passed through Samaria. Like them, the Samaritans suffered oppression. They also cherished hatred against the Roman tax collectors. Still they chortled with glee when they saw the men of Israel march by. Clearly it also went hard with them under Roman rule. They perceived that Ben Nesher's troop came in rebellion and marched to meet their doom. That did the Samaritans good, and whenever the Jews disappeared far enough upon the rugged road they seized rocks and smote Ben Nesher's men from behind.

The following day they left behind the land over which Herod Antipas seemingly reigned and along a small grey valley they came upon the first slopes of the highlands of Judea. Ever more partisans joined the small army of Ben Nesher which had halted near a place called Noema. The commander knew that the caravan of a tax collector from northern Judea would stop in that village overnight. He wanted to attack.

Groups of men lay on the ridges and in the hollows of the barren grey mountains. Eagles that saw them screamed and abandoned their nests. Some of the rebels peered at the predatory birds with amazement. Curious vultures did not remain so aloof. They hovered over the mountain tops and alighted on overhanging rocks. Then they stretched out their naked necks and their red eyes stared at the solitary men of Israel. Some of the men rubbed themselves against the rocks, for their backs itched from hunger and insect bites. Sitting by himself on a large rock, Menachem gazed at the army of outlaws. There were fathers of families from Jerusalem, farmers from the plain of Esdrelon, Pharisees that for long years had joyfully prayed in the synagogues and ragged youths from Transjordan and Perea, sea fishermen, young lads who had run away from the schools of the Law, Levites in rags who found no more joy in their Temple. Some slept on the ridge.

He saw a couple who had placed massive Roman swords upon their abdomens. The weapons moved up and down with their breathing. Some lay on their bellies and cupped their heads in the hands like boys. They slept like the thirsty who drink and the lovers who mate. Their own lives passed by whether they slept or kept watch. A network of tiny streams was diverted to their aim: to uproot the Romans and eject them from the land! Was their purpose God's purpose? Or was God's design precisely the work that did not matter anymore: to eat a good meal the following day, to see a wife in Jericho again, to bless a child or hear Rabbi Gamaliel explain the Torah? Some slept on their sides with rocks in their loins. And there were those who stared at the stars with open eyes. They sent out thoughts of longing or love like a polyp its unwitting tentacles or a plant its unwitting roots. They did not know that they were floating with the stream. Floating or drifting away on the tide. That we never know.

6

EARLY MORNING THE ORDER came to break camp. Ben Nesher had the motto of the hidden leader Yehuda the Galilean repeated from group to group: "He who serves the Romans offends God." And they set out to plunder.

The men were unequally armed. Some had nothing in their hands nor on their backs. Others wore Roman shields on their arms. Many had axes. The axe suited those who wield it for felling rotten tree trunks.

They proceeded along the valley whilst above, along the mountain ridges, black figures were climbing. Sometimes these black figures made almost no headway, then all at once they advanced with speed. They were the scouts. When one saw a speck in the distance or a moving line in the heights, one became aware of man's helplessness and puniness as well as a certain exaltation. The solitary figure represented one of God's dice which had rolled down.

The rhythm of marching feet on rocky ground blended with the metallic clang of weapons. Everything in Ben Nesher's roving band was fiercer than the equivalent of its intended prey, the tax caravan: escorts, weapons and will. Relentlessly the rebels stalked the sun-scorched, dusty caravan with its precious cargo.

The men above gave the signal. They thrust their weapons in the air and waved them to and fro. Ben Nesher divided his army into columns that would scale the mountains in order to penetrate the village on three fronts. No paths crossed these mountains—the scouts girded ropes around their middle in order to haul up their comrades. Menachem remained with Ben Nesher's column. The ascent proved painful as the random features of the rocky cliffs challenged their endurance. Sweat poured down their grimy faces and formed streaks in their hair. Initially Ben Nesher's column saw their comrades climbing from afar. Although the ascent seemed like child's play from a distance, the obstacles of the terrain frustrated the climbers.

Harnessing his agility, Ben Nesher gained a foothold on a higher ledge, gripped a jutting rock, pulled himself up and said: "We're on our way." The target beckoned beyond the next ridge which they crossed after what appeared to be an endless struggle. Moving swiftly now with weapons at the ready, they approached the town.

Their target, the caravan they pursued so single-mindedly, had already broken up to find resting places throughout the town. Near the first row of houses lay the camels. The ground around the beasts was occupied by bags heaped high. Idumeans, Arabs, Africans and even a sprinkling of men from the nations of Yaphet—all of them armed with spears—guarded the beasts and their valuable cargo.

A spy of Ben Nesher's reported to him that the Roman tax collector had spent the night in one of the town's few large houses whilst other Romans lay resting on the roofs to prepare for the next stage of their journey.

Ben Nesher awaited the arrival of his two other columns. The second one soon met up with his rear guard as it entered the town from the back behind a row of houses. Then he gave the order to attack.

Shouting "For Freedom and Israel!" the partisans fell upon the enemy. As Ben Nesher's group headed for the camels, a dark youth saw them advancing like a pack of predators and screamed: "The tigers of Yehuda the Galilean!"

So formidable was the free army that the mere mention of its name had the effect of paralyzing the tax guards. Flinging their spears to the ground they gave themselves up without a fight. The men of Ben Nesher's second column stormed the houses, smashing down doors and falling on the small number of Romans that had demanded shelter inside. Some avenged themselves personally by hurling Romans from the roofs. The axe of Israel's avengers dangled menacingly over the vacillating Jews.

"Are you obedient to God or to Rome?" growled Ben Nesher's men. For some these words evoked profound emotions in the soul. For others they meant nothing more than the stones in their hands. Woe to the Jew who in his anguish attempted to provide a long explanation. Before he had finished his brains had spattered from his skull.

Ben Nesher permitted the homes of the Roman slaves and the Herodian Jews to be sacked although no one could keep personal booty for himself. Everything gained was for the support of the free army's immediate needs.

Opposite Ben Nesher stood the commander of the convoy, a slender Latin from northern Italy.

"What do you demand of me?" asked the enemy.

"I want nothing from you—I only take back what is ours."

"You offend Caesar. Beware what you do."

"You offend God on his own soil, idolator. This entire land is a Holy Temple. The stranger who steps on it with unhallowed feet must die."

"Would you murder me?"

"I shall slay you. We desperately needed help, Roman. We had closed an alliance with you. We asked for your assistance. Like fools we opened the gates and welcomed you. You came, you entered, you saw. Once inside, you defiled the Temple. To you, only two things hold meaning: power and gold!"

"Have mercy!" cried the Roman.

"In Jerusalem they sacrifice goats and bulls, poor animals that could never cause offence to God—I sacrifice a thief who came as a friend!"

"Mercy!"

"This land has been bled dry of mercy."

Menachem saw Ben Nesher fling down his axe. His large hands caught the Roman by the throat and smashed his skull against the room's stone wall.

"It is better to die than to kill like that!" exclaimed Menachem.

"You know not how much Israel has suffered!" the leader snarled at him.

Three men dashed in panting.

"Ben Nesher, we are betrayed!"

"What's going on!?"

"There is a man arrived from the third column to warn us. The column of Reuben the Perean has been taken."

"Then they must have known about our plans," muttered Ben Nesher. "Either that or they expected an attack somewhere along the route. How dumb I was; this operation was too obvious. How many enemies are there?"

"They speak of two legions from Varus."

"There are only two ways out," Ben Nesher declared while looking at Menachem. "God still keeps one of them closed. The other one is good too."

"Death?" asked Menachem.

"Death!" affirmed Ben Nesher. They went outside, their weapons drawn. Ben Nesher's men formed a close formation like a herd of bulls shaking horns, eager to fight. No one seemed afraid. They had been surprised in the process of performing their work. Brave and ready to die, Ben Nesher's men stood their ground as they had always kept their feet on the ground even when aspiring to the heights. Menachem had seen much discord in Israel but never such unity. The block of warriors on the road resembled a fortress. They knew why Jacob had set out for Canaan.

The Romans—all of them regular troops—surged closer. Sabinus the proconsul had pressed Varus in Syria to dispatch them to Judea. Along the way its commanders were informed that Yehuda's men intended to strike. Led by centurions and a commander-in-chief, the army wearing Roman helmets approached with rhythmic step. The vanguard consisted of missile slingers wearing light sandals. The spearmen with shields on the breast came next, followed by armored troops in third place.

"Duck!" yelled Ben Nesher to his center men around him. They stooped, raised again their fortress armed with heavy stones that they flung at the enemy across their own ranks. A cloud of small sharp stones struck up and down. Some lost an eye through them. The Romans, regular like a wave, were now close by. A hail of darts descended on the partisans that waited with spears and axes at the ready.

"Accursed fools, give yourselves up!" called the Roman commander. Safe in the midst of his men, he wore a rich overcoat over his tunic.

"To whom? To wolf cubs?" sneered Ben Nesher.

Then the main body of Romans attacked while others marched out to encircle the rebels. They hacked at each other as though they were demolishing houses. Axes, spears and swords stuck fast to ribs or split skulls. They bounced against bones, sunk deep into human flesh. Ben Nesher who towered above the rest, shattered the shoulders of many Romans with his battle-axe that day. Menachem forced himself to think of the slaughter in Nazareth and Israel's future. Somehow there must still be a way. A way that was more righteous than sinful.

He heard himself muttering: "Thou shalt not murder—Thou shalt not murder," and each time he said it, he thrust his dagger in the throat of an enemy, in the shoulder, in the belly, even once under the eye. "Thou shalt not murder." What was it that made men blaspheme this commandment in God's world? The perversity of sin. Would he ever reach the other side, would Israel ever reach the other side, would humanity someday arrive on the other side of sin, where there was no more murder? Menachem, one of the supplest, stooped, crawled between the legs of the combatants and plunged his dagger in the groins of a man who was battling Ben Nesher with his sword.

"Ben Nesher, do you still have strength?"

"Always! From Judah Maccabee to the end of time!" shouted the leader. His love for Israel was so great that he wished to drill a hole through destiny until he reached Nothingness or the Day of Judgment.

"He knows what it means to be chosen. He is spotted with sin but a hero of God," thought Menachem. But then a Roman sword knocked the axe from Ben Nesher's hand. There was a breach in the fortress. The Roman could have slain him then. Menachem darted to one side of the enemy and stuck a dagger in his throat.

"You fight well, Menachem!" cried Ben Nesher.

"In order to get it over," shouted Menachem. "I fight as many live, in order to be done with it!"

Afterwards he fell. The flat side of a sword had brought him down.

The men from Judea and Galilee had fought with the audacity of he-goats and the tenacity of bulls. It seemed as though they would gain the victory and even carry off the gold extorted by the Roman censor. But a singular crackling roar that approached put an end to their confidence. Their efforts had been in vain once more. The Roman infantry was accompanied by a regiment of cavalry. This wing had concealed itself in the mountain pass. Now they thundered forth. Horses' hooves are of much harder stuff than human bodies. Their hooves can kill a man with one blow. And the riders sit high and slay the foot soldiers from above. Oh, fighting people of Israel, your eternal adversary is overwhelming force!

"Yield or we cut you to pieces," yelled the first rider.

"Go ahead!" scoffed Ben Nesher who still stood among the survivors.

"It proves nothing! Jackals devour the corpse of the prophet and then raise a leg to pee on his beard."

"Attack!"

The men of Yehuda the Galilean did not fall back. They hurled themselves forward and continued to hack the horses' legs with their axes while the Roman riders split their heads and the crashing horses knocked them down. But only the first rows succeeded in dying so.

The Roman commanders had ordered their men to take alive as many rebels as possible. Above all, Ben Nesher himself was of special value to them. The cavalry thus encircled the group of surviving rebels and attempted to cast ropes around their necks. Suddenly the order "Pisces"—fish—resounded. In an instant an enormously wide net was cast, which the horsemen skillfully unfurled over the heads of Ben Nesher's men. A swarm of enemies then poured over the crumpled and fallen men. And the conquerors, proud of their successful maneuver, shouted: "Victory, victory!"

In truth, many more Romans died there that day when they tried to disarm and bind the rebels. But long rows of Israel's avengers, with manacled hands and a broader chain around their ankles, marched southward surrounded by Roman soldiers and slave drivers with horse whips. When night approached they were allowed to rest on the stones. Their chains jangled on the rocks. The Romans kindled fires and ate roast meat and bread. A few had orders to shove bread crusts into the prisoners' mouths. Another went around with a stone jar, and Ben Nesher's men set their thick dry lips to it and sipped a draught. Then they collapsed. The chains jingled again. They felt their ankles and wrists burning and a heavy bell pounding inside their heads.

Menachem awoke. It is good that it happened, he thought, but did it have to happen? And if Yehuda the Galilean and Ben Nesher and the others had not risen to resist the Romans? Then would we be wasting away in impotence. The Romans have vowed our destruction. What does it matter whether we are destroyed by Ben Nesher's violence, by the folded hands of Abba the Pharisee or the closed eye of the Essenes? Such as we are, we must suffer, but we shall not perish. We will be reborn in another form. Such indeed is God's will.

In every generation there is a deluge over Israel, and in every generation a Noah's ark.

He heard a man who rolled over beside him groaning: "Imathi, Imathi!" He was calling his mother. Another, opposite him, tugged at his manacled hands and tried afterwards to slide on his belly, but he could not because the chains pressed too hard against the bones of his flesh. Ben Nesher saw that the man wished to masturbate in order to steal a few seconds of joy in the night of his misfortune. It did not succeed and the man cried out: "Damn it, not even that!"

Then Menachem prayed: "For the sake of the thirty righteous men God suffers entire generations to exist! For the sake of the thirty righteous ones God should have destroyed humanity. Have pity, extinguish them, oh Lord. Yet even the good who are oppressed wish to live, Israel seeks the light, the widow does not desire death, and after the death of their parents the orphans stand at the window to watch the sun coming up.

I know not! Job, the pious one, knew not! The suffering wish to live, the good are ready to enter upon evil ways, if only they may live. They beget children for their own comfort in this world and their children beget other children to indemnify themselves for the affliction which their parents have done to them by conceiving them. Mankind has chosen between being and non-being. If you do not suffer us to exist out of love, then you must surely do it out of pity for our attachment to life. Oh, God, for the hundredth time I ask Your Mercy for Israel and for the miserable people who would rather be evil than dead and who would rather behold evil than Your glory! For I understand it not."

7

THE FOLLOWING DAY THEY went further. With burning feet and swollen legs they were marched over the highways of their own land under the watchful eye of the strangers.

"Where are we going?" clamored a couple when a Roman captain rode by.

The officer smiled. "It is a secret. Rejoice. We are going to your Jerusalem."

Some died on the way. Now and then an eagle screamed and cranes flew by, uttering their trumpet cries. Sometimes a cow lowed. From time to time Menachem heard someone scream: "Shema Yisrael!" and then something like a death rattle as one of the avengers sagged to the ground. And still their destiny dragged them on with rattling chains. Some kept their eyes shut. For to see inwardly was much more important to them than to see outwardly.

"Why must people despise each other?" thought Menachem. "The townsmen despise the men of violence. Even my friend Yeshua scorned these avengers. But to drudge in chains over burning roads is heavy work. My comrades bear Israel. I see a long, long ark. Even though their hands are bound and their arms hang limply, they carry the Holy Ark. They have still other arms that are raised aloft. The palms of their hands lie flat. They carry the tabernacle. They carry God. They too."

And Menachem walked on. His power of endurance was great. He looked at the man beside him. The latter had a sword cut over one cheek. The wound was swollen with clotted blood. This made him look like a rapacious feline.

"They will sell us as slaves!" said Menachem to his neighbor.

"Do you believe that? They will crucify us!"

"Tell us, what would you still like to see once before you die?" called a Galilean in front of them, a bearded man of forty.

"I would like to celebrate Passover in Jerusalem. How good it would be if I could bless the wine. Bore peri ha-gafen."

"Amen," chanted the others, and they smiled.

"Stiff-necked fools," a Roman officer shouted to a comrade.

"These people live on words!" answered the centurion. "They fight us because of a couple of words. They get intoxicated on words."

"A little faster, you laggards. You are going to Jerusalem. You will arrive too late for the sacrifices."

"When a Roman sacrifices, God pinches his nose tightly," yelled a peasant from the Syrian border.

They arrived in the vicinity of Jerusalem. The roads were better built and full of people. Camel caravans, drivers with asses, a lady in a sedan chair, women with water pitchers on their heads and men with yokes over their shoulders came past. They were free. Heaven and hell passed each other frequently on God's earth.

Some pedestrians remained standing, staring after the chained men. They saw that they were Jews, captured rebels.

"May God give you strength!" an old woman called out to each group that marched past her. Out of respect for the prisoners she did not move until the whole procession had passed by. Most of the men looked at them stealthily. Where Romans were involved there was always danger.

Life in the capital city was rich and full but the captives had nothing more to do with the rose-tinted existence which their wives, children and villages still continued to pursue. They were pushed through the city like a thread through a needle. They passed women too. The prisoners called to them with sweet or obscene names.

A young woman with a black kerchief over her head and shoulders shortened her step so she could keep close to Menachem. He was already long gone from the free world and marveled when she spoke his name.

"Menachem!"

"Is it you, Yocheved?"

"It is I."

"How did you know I was here?"

"I have run away from home. My mother has gone after a lover, my father to find the Law. May I not go then after my friend? I asked in all places where Ben Nesher had passed."

She remained silent and tried to keep equal pace with Menachem. Then she said: "I want to be with you, Menachem. Let me be with you, whether you live or die!"

"It cannot be!"

"Why not?"

"See you not that I walk in a row?"

"I shall go along with you, Menachem. Each word of yours torments me. Last night when I crossed the road I dreamt of you. You were a prince, Menachem, and you were going away. You exchanged your clothes with those of a beggar. You told me that you wished to find poverty in exile. I said that I would redeem you. Then there came a sort of luminous being, an angel, who cried out to me: 'That cannot be, Yocheved. For Menachem will lose his wealth on his own.'"

"I know that well, Malach,"[1] was my reply. "Menachem is being pushed into poverty and exile by the hand of Goodness. But if Goodness does me harm, then is he evil. I hate him and shall redeem Menachem."

A long silence followed.

"Go now, Yocheved. You have been my beloved from days that are not allotted to me."

"I go, Menachem but I shall never relinquish you."

She turned away from Menachem and then hastened her step imperceptibly so that she went before the line of prisoners in the direction of Jerusalem. Her steps corresponded to the rhythm of those words, "I must save him, I must save him."

Menachem had spoken truthfully. She knew that he was consumed by Israel. She found him too beautiful for his calling but not too beautiful for herself. Why did no word of tenderness come from his lips? Why did he not embrace her? Then she said to herself:

"My father did it not, my mother did it not, my friend does it not. Yocheved, I love you, your black hair is soft when my fingers caress it. Your dark eyes are so full of promise in your calm, radiant face but it is the serenity of passion. Oh Yocheved, I love you so much. If only I could rock you like a child. So I comfort myself. I have to declare my love to myself. I must save him, I must save him, I must save him! For myself? I must save him even if at the price of death. I cannot cease thinking of myself but I can give up life. If I keep afflicting myself with my own needs I shall die. Menachem, Menachem, Menachem, by day and by night! I must save him and I will!"

"Come you tonight to lie with me, my dove?" a Roman officer called to her.

---

1. Angel, messenger.

"That will I do if you let Menachem go free, idolator. First will I try something else. A woman may only play the harlot when love has driven her to despair."

"When come you to my tent, oh beautiful Jerusalemite? Your breasts are more lovely than the mountains of Lebanon!"

"Why do you make sport of our songs, idolator? I will even lie with you if you set Menachem free. Why not with you? But first I will try other means. I still love my body too much not to grieve for it afterwards. A woman may only whore when her body is worth nothing more to her. Then she must smile at men who will still give her a drachma for it. Oh Menachem, what would I not do to free you from the Romans, from Israel and from Goodness. I must save him!"

Yocheved removed the kerchief from her head as she entered her father's house which had a wide façade with twelve windows on the first floor of its perimeter. Abba Alexander kept his home in good order but he himself occupied only a small portion; he lived in a tiny room behind the gallery. Yocheved entered and remained standing until he raised his eyes from the parchment scroll he was reading. He must have seen her because under his reading he said:

"You have returned, my wayward daughter. The times are not such that I can punish you. I must busy myself with greater things. When the branches are rotten the trunk may not break. What is it?"

"Father, give me money—much money: ten talents. I have need of it forthwith."

"Why?"

"For Menachem!"

"For the son of the merchant? What is he to me?"

"He is everything to your daughter!"

"How can I know that? His father has never said anything to me and he himself has never spoken of it to me. He can mean nothing to my daughter."

"He is everything to me!"

As he got up, Abba Alexander turned pale and his black eyes started flashing.

"I am old and avoid the street. Has it come to this then that the daughters of Judea draw near to whoever calls them?"

"Speak no folly. Have you never heard of love?" asked Yocheved.

"Aye, and of responsibility. God bless lasting love!" Abba replied.

"What do you call lasting? For a man to run off with a woman?"

"Taking up your responsibility as a wife," he retorted.

"I love this man. What have you against him?"

"I have nothing against him except that I know him not. Why has he not come here to me? The vacant space in this house is the result of your mother's love. People who take love so lightly give themselves the right to abandon one sweetheart for another. There are clouds over Israel, Yocheved. I shall not always be here to protect you. Beware of the love of a man who does not desire you. Why has he not come here?"

"Father, I beg for ransom money. The man is in the hands of the Romans. He was with Ben Nesher's troop. I wish to redeem him."

A change came over Abba Alexander's face.

"God expects us to ransom prisoners. Go and when you learn what the idolator demands, come tell me. The soul of Menachem ben Gedalia rests now upon me. You have named him."

"Father, I understand you not. Is a soul in Israel worth more than Yocheved's love?"

"I know now the prisoner but not your lover. I do not wish to know him. When I know what they ask and I have the money, I shall buy myself blessings and may perform a good deed."

8

OUTSIDE JERUSALEM MANY MOUNTAINS rose up against one another to overshadow the valleys between them, rendering them insignificant. It was here that Ben Nesher's men had been brought. On these slopes the short and menacing crosses were already being erected.

In the darkness two Roman soldiers crept closer and groped for Menachem's feet. He lay half dozing, exhausted by hunger. "Scream not, Jew. You have been ransomed. A woman waits for you there."

One of the soldiers crawled higher up on his belly until he lay beside Menachem and touched his wrist. Menachem felt a disagreeable sensation. He had no desire for liberation. "Why do they have to ransom me?" he thought. "Why do they break my shackles?" I was safe with my comrades. They cannot break our chains." But when the soldiers had done their work the woman already stood before him. In the moonlight she looked like a small, exquisite mountain cone. Yocheved had drawn closer because she had foreseen that Menachem would not wish to come. Although she did not think like he did, her love gave her the words that fitted his character like a key.

"Menachem, get up! Come with me. It is I, Yocheved. Father has ransomed you. You are free so you may continue to wear the chains of your choice."

"They will crucify my comrades and I shall not be with them."

"You will see many crucified, and you will be there, and it will never end for you because you love them so much. Come, go with me, I beseech you. We have ransomed you for service, for the avodah,[1] says my father. Come Menachem; let not your pity for your comrades of yesterday turn you aside from your duty to your companions of tomorrow. If you can live, you must live. I swear it to you by God and Israel."

"You love me truly, Yocheved. You speak not your words but mine."

1. Sacrifice.

She begged him on her knees. Then he arose in order to lift her up and went swiftly away with her, shame-faced like a thief. With his arms around her waist he ran with her down the mountain slope and through the valley towards a new path which led upward again. It was beginning to turn grey between the mountains to the north of Jerusalem and in the light came the rosy wrinkles on the forehead of dawn. Then blue sky filled the gaps between the mountains. Yocheved was overjoyed but she did not wish to let it be seen, for Menachem thought, "If I rejoice in the dawn today, I may be accursed."

They entered Jerusalem through the gate of Ephraim. On the edge among the narrow streets it already became apparent that an uncommonly heated day was in store for the feverish city. Especially in the vicinity of the Temple many people were stirring. They formed groups. Black bearded men walked vehemently to and fro. Their beards were cubed, the weight of their manhood displayed on their chins. In the groups also stood aged men with white beards and women with kerchiefs over their hair.

"Woe is us, what is now again over Israel?" a couple exclaimed. They were women of forty-five who had borne and reared children and who were now witnessing the birth pangs of time in Israel's womb. Some young men stood apart from the groups. Their mouths looked grim; a few laughed derisively when a greybeard spoke. Among them were Sicarii who carried daggers under their cloaks. When a man in the crowds urged great prudence, glossing over the deeds of the proconsul, the wearer of the sica would follow him perhaps to thrust the dagger in his bosom at a street corner.

Menachem and Yocheved soon learned why the people were in uproar. The new proconsul called Pontius Pilate, a thief like his predecessors, had caused great offense. Flags bearing the image of Caesar Tiberius in the likeness of a god had been erected next to the Temple. And now five thousand men had come to protest.

"Big wigs!" mocked a young man. "They will accomplish nothing. Words, beards, gestures. Meanwhile the idolator thinks of the hips of his last wife and of the letter which must be on the way to Rome."

Yocheved and Menachem made their way to the house of Abba Alexander in Beth-Zeta, the wealthy quarter. They did not find Abba at home however and learned from a servant that the old Pharisee formed part of the delegation which the people had sent to the proconsul. Mollified by these tidings, Yocheved told her friend:

"Father is not wicked. He will even court death for his idle fancies. Let us go to him. It is indeed a great time, Menachem, every walk we take may be our last one. Each encounter the last time that one sees an acquaintance. God keeps himself sorely occupied with his people Israel. Don't you find it so, Menachem? On account of being chosen, perhaps?"

"Because we are chosen," replied Menachem. "How can he demonstrate it otherwise? By coddling us with honey cake or by having other people bow to his beloved?" Yocheved found no answer.

They came to the middle of a great concourse of people near the palace of the proconsul behind the Tower of David. The forecourt of the palace was surrounded by walls. But the men climbed on each other's shoulders and from there onto the wall. The delegates from Jerusalem, mostly Pharisees, stood waiting in the yard. They had come to implore the proconsul to remove the image of Caesar from near the Temple.

Answer they had not received. But they might not depart or perhaps they did not wish to go away and waited with great patience. Some turned around and looked up at the spectators on the wall. Then they shook their heads sadly and raised their hands only to let them fall again. It had lasted two days already.

The proconsul Pontius Pilate appeared before one of the small windows of the palace. He grinned when he saw the Jews. "They are like good-natured buffaloes," he said. "Some are still standing on their legs. Others lie already in their excrement." He beckoned to a captain.

"Rufus Gratus?"

"Here I am, master."

"Dispatch now the soldiers against these oxen. If they do not leave immediately, slay them. Tell them that Pontius Pilate after due deliberation has finally found a just answer."

A row of archers followed by soldiers with spears and swords sallied forth from the tiny doorway of a basement. Another group of two hundred foot soldiers stormed around the corner to the courtyard in double time. These had camped on a side of the place where the Jews could not discover them. Then fifty armored horsemen trotted out into the yard on Arabian steeds. The five thousand pious men from Jerusalem gave way. A mounted herald blew his horn. Another took a papyrus, unrolled it and cried out:

"Command of the proconsul of our divine Caesar Tiberius. The Jews must disperse at once. Their request is denied and is considered an affront to the Caesars. Those who remain will be killed on the spot. Go!"

The riders still restrained their horses. The spearmen advanced one knee and thrust their lances straight in front of them. The archers drew their strings. The gate of the inner courtyard was opened wide. But the Jews did not leave through the open gate. One after the other they bared their throat and chest and lay down on the ground. The gestures of the men, one after the other, recalled the tiny flames in the candelabra during the freedom feast of Chanukah. Eight little flames were kindled one after the other.

Old Abba Alexander also wished to lie down. He was a heavily built man and he panted from the effort of bending his knees. His heart thumped in his bosom. Once on his knees he let himself fall sideways. He smiled though his thick cheeks. Isaac, his role model, lay down easier in his supple youth when he stretched himself out on the altar in anticipation of the sacrificial knife.

The old ringleader, Samuel ben Berachya who had remained standing in front of the others ran up to the horse of the Roman herald.

"We depart not. We want no images of false gods in Jerusalem. You can kill us." Then the old man also lay down in front of the horse. Pontius Pilate watched this spectacle pensively from his window.

"Did I not say so? Now all the buffaloes lie in their filth."

It was a singular sight to see thousands of men lying there on their backs with uncovered chests.

"Why did they not send their wives?"

Colorful too was that butcher's field of the living, for the one had a red, another a brown and a third a blue mantle.

Then the proconsul reminded himself that precisely this evening he had to send a letter to Rome. He thoughtfully stroked his brow. He had witnessed a singular spectacle. Why should he get involved in potentially great trouble for nothing? He had more than enough enemies in Rome. His continued absence was a danger in itself. He would call off the feast.

Menachem and Yocheved entered through the open gate. "See you my father?" Yocheved clutched his arm.

"There are thousands here."

Nevertheless, by chance as it were, he saw the old man lying like a fallen animal, ready for the knife of the ritual butcher. Menachem had never found old Abba Alexander so ludicrous yet so sublime as when he was lying there like an overturned barrel with the divine spirit blazing inside of him. He wanted to run to him and replace him on his pedestal of dignity. Sad indeed is a man without that pedestal, for his soul has departed like a mollusk from its shell.

"Are they not fools?" a slender man asked Yocheved, perhaps in order to make contact with the beautiful woman. "They make uproar because of a couple of images of Caesar in the city."

"The road back is swift," answered Menachem. "Are you a Sadducee or perchance a Greek?"

"No madman in either case," retorted the elegantly dressed man.

"Come Yocheved, I go to help your father."

"What did you mean by 'The road back is swift,' Menachem?"

"For two thousand years we could not wait for God and we panted for the image of a false idol. Our forefathers made the Golden Calf. Now we can await God forever and are willing to die so as not to behold the image of a false god. I believe that is what is called progress, Yocheved. But surely one thing I know: that the road ahead is much more difficult than the way back."

"Was the Sadducee not right then?" she replied pouting. "But today I love my father. I don't want him to die. Is it worth the effort to perish for a couple of images in Jerusalem?"

"God is quickly belittled, Yocheved. It cost us so much effort to let Him span heaven and earth. Look, the worst is over. The soldiers are marching off; counter orders have come. I go to help your father up. I love him because of his daughter, and I love his daughter because of her father."

"Today, Menachem, you love me only today."

"When shall it happen again, Yocheved? Is a peaceful day in Israel a respite from misfortune, or a year of unrest and murder a reprieve from blessings? Do you know?"

He shook his head sadly. Then they went to Abba Alexander, kneeled down beside him, gripped the man by the arms and pulled him to his feet.

Menachem left them to visit his mother's house. This also stood in the new quarter which was names after the olive tree. It was large and built in the Roman fashion. In front of the house, which was separated from another by a large garden, lay a low row of dromedaries calmly chewing their spittle through crossed lips. Menachem ran into the garden and found the rooms on the ground floor empty. His mother was frail and in her ways younger than he. A graceful chalice in which many tears fell. Menachem entered her room.

The furniture—a table, chair, divan and lamps still stood there. Rachel threw herself into his arms and cried out, "I did not know whether you were still alive! A woman came to tell me that you had been taken prisoner. She swore she would save you. I was so afraid I to lose you, Menachem." She stroked her fingers through his thick, lanky, black hair. "I did not want to lose you but I rejoiced that you had gone away with our oppressed and suffering people."

For a moment there was silence. Then she resumed in a tone of embarrassment: "My household is broken up."

"I saw it, mother. I saw a caravan of dromedaries in front of the house. The guards lie nearby."

"Your father is leaving for good, Menachem. He is taking everything with him. Only I remain behind, poor, a woman rejected."

"What will you do?"

"Wait. The same that our people do: wait. But I can wait for my death. The people cannot wait and they will erupt in violence. And no one can hinder it. Sometimes I ask myself whether God bides His time until these people can wait no longer and perform an insane deed which will lead to their downfall. When I was a girl I lived in a village in Samaria. A young lion hunted in the neighborhood and killed many cattle. The men from the village wanted to catch him. They built a pit for him. The lamb which was to decoy the lion was already bound and lay in the pit. I lay with my brother in ambush in order to see what would happen. For a long time the lion ran away from the pit. Then he lay down nearby waiting for the lamb to come out. For hours long we waited. At last he could not wait any longer and jumped into the pit. I think that God uses the same device in order to bring a person and a people to its destiny. I remain waiting. Your father has said that I may remain living in my room and keep the furniture. He wishes to rent our house to others and will ask the new inhabitants not to drive me from my room."

"I am weary mother and wish to sleep. Towards the fall of evening I go away. Be not uneasy. I shall return quickly."

"Go rest, my son. Lie down on this couch and take this pillow under your head."

When her son slept she sighed half-aloud: "Awake, Menachem. Even though you watch over our people you can avert nothing, for all roads lead to the same end. Shomer, ma mi layla, ma mi layil?"[2]

In the night Menachem arose cautiously. He understood that Rachel only feigned to be asleep but he respected her pretense and slipped out of the room and the house. He headed in a westerly direction, crossed the city garden and saw the slender silhouette of the Roman bath house looming up. Then he stole swiftly through the narrow steep street, the final offshoot of the temple quarter in the heart of the city. The Jerusalemites had become afraid of night. Darkness was a cooking pot. Every new morning the dawn knocked the lid off. At night events were brewed and cast into history. God plotted events in the night. The Romans plotted events in the night. The Zealots plotted events in the night. Therefore later generations sang:

Vayehi bechatsi halayla—"and it came to pass at midnight."

Their steps gave warning of an approaching Roman troop of twenty. How arrogantly they trod on the ancient stones—who could be more ignorant than the masters of the hour? Menachem slipped into a dark doorway waiting for the soldiers to pass. Upon emerging, he saw others who had hidden themselves make their appearance here and there. The manner in which people lived these days was a return to something bestial. Might these men be patriots preparing another act of violence? If so, all Jews in Jerusalem would suffer for it tomorrow. Maybe the patriots acted in memory of their forefathers; the Romans could not make them pay any more. Perhaps they performed their deeds in devotion to this generation's remote descendants over whom the Romans had no power either. What good could come out of their deeds now? Yet, the results may be revealed at the end of days!

Ben Nesher's comrades were lost but their seed was already discharged in time. How many days, how many centuries would pass before the new men awoke? Would God be able to discern the difference between hours and centuries, that distinction which is everything to an individual?

Menachem had now arrived outside the city. Like a solitary beast he climbed the heights and descended from the ridges. At last he reached a valley filled with night beyond which a mountain slope rose up towards the light of many torches burning on the summit. Many wounds and souls were also burning there. Menachem saw from the valley a pitiful grove of short trees that were all alike, having a horizontal branch across the trunk. They

2. "Watchman, what of the night?"

were the crosses waiting patiently until the crucified men would pass away in the world of whirling dust. They were Menachem's comrades from the partisan troop of Ben Nesher.

Now Menachem made himself flat like a stalking panther. Thus he climbed, arms folded to the elbow, dragging his feet and knee caps up the slope until he drew near to the camp of the dying. Not all the crosses were visible since the night obscured them. Only where the torches and faggots burnt brightly did the flames reveal the tortured body, broken neck and head of a brave warrior of yesterday.

Five or six dying men were still visible in the grim light but their features were difficult to distinguish. The slope resembled a garden with paths. A Roman guard patrolled the area with an air of indifference. The Romans were not yet linked with humanity in the way that Israel was. How could they sense that their equals were dying here? It was difficult to discover Ben Nesher in that fitfully exposed darkness. Just as the black panther glides after its prey, so Menachem slid further up the heights and until he recognized his friend Ben Nesher in the flickering light.

The Romans loved geometrical figures. The rows of crosses diminished in number from the base to the top of the hill. The highest rows numbered only ten crosses. Above these rows Ben Nesher hung alone on a massive tree trunk. Menachem crept further up and slid into a hollow pit near the crucified warrior. He raised his head to take a long look at the martyred rebel. Ben Nesher appeared even more enormous in the light which shot out tiny flames like striking vipers. His large aquiline nose divided his sunken cheeks like an impotent weapon above earth and mankind. His shrunken feet and his powerful hands were nailed flat on the wood. Those bloodied hands and feet were proof of mankind" debasement. They were the sturdy laboring hands and feet of Adam. Menachem moved closer until he lay directly before Ben Nesher's cross and called his name. The patriot's eyes opened. Menachem thought that they opened wider than before, wider than their limits. Before they had been commanding and hard. Now they were melancholy. They wanted to draw the whole world inside. Why do innocent people die so? Do they wish to call the whole world as witness?

"Ben Nesher, do you hear me?"

"I hear you, Menachem."

"Ben Nesher, do you know why I do not die beside you?"

"I know Menachem. The future, the future. We can only serve her at this time if we all do it in different ways."

"Ben Nesher, in God's name forgive me if I pierce your dying heart with a question: Do you still believe in your way?"

"Aye, Menachem. I have chosen the good road for God and Israel. . . . The journey is not yet over."

How difficult it is to find one single way which is appropriate for all people, for Israel and for a crucified humanity, thought Menachem.

"I have chosen the good road," continued the exhausted man on the cross with a strong voice.

"They dragged away my son before the eyes of his mother, and they taunted her and said they would make a eunuch of him. They burned the village where I was born to the ground. I understood then that my son was Israel, that my village was Israel, that every word we speak and every field we plough is Israel. I became an avenger. But I say to you, Menachem, that this is a false word. What have I to avenge? Nothing and no one. Vengeance is for the idolators that look to the past. Israel is the future. I am no avenger. I am one who brings forth the future. I do not want history to repeat. I do not want them to make eunuchs of our sons. Is that not good? What else does God want Israel to do then? Either this cross is folly or God does not exist. God fills heaven and earth so this cross means nothing. It does not symbolize my transgression but my righteousness. If Israel is not free then God is not free. He may command the storm and the thunder, He may rule over the stars of infinity, but if upon this earth Israel is not free and the Romans remain masters, then God is not free either and mankind is his master.

I die contented, Menachem. My feet are bloody but they have walked the good road. Our road leads either to a destination or there is no end and if so, the rule of the Romans will also never end. I am not afraid. God is imprisoned in mankind only for as long as He Himself wills it. Woe betide them, Israel lives!"

Then arose the ghost of Samson before Ben Nesher. He saw himself standing blinded in the idolator temple. He strained his mighty muscles. He flung his arms around the pillars of the idolator temple and the stone structure collapsed on his enemies and himself. The veins on Ben Nesher's forehead bulged. His nose appeared like the beak of an eagle about to shut over the men that crucified his people. Spasms shot through his arms to his wrists. Again he tortured his own hands and feet by tensing his body like the string of a bow, the bow being his cross. The wounds where the nails pierced his body were consumed by scorching pain. One last time he speared his body at hands and feet.

Menachem watched Ben Nesher's countenance turn pale. The exertion was followed by surrender. His head hung only by the vertebrae. His eyes were already closed. Ben Nesher was dead and Menachem hoped that he lay with Samson under the ruins of the idolator temple.

Menachem did not sneak away from the hill of torture. He stood up and ran down the paths in the garden of crosses. It felt as if he soared in huge leaps over the dead, away from the scene of inhumanity.

The sun rose over Jerusalem. Men dared to go out in the street again. They stood timid and yearning before each new day, as a bashful maiden would before a young man in his prime.

Why could the new day not be God's day?

But the Roman soldiers were there, marching through the city while the palace of the proconsul towered over all. The new day was a treasure trove offering enough light from dawn till dusk. History, however, with her wagon-loads of misery formed part of the new day too as it stood waiting at the gates of Jerusalem. The maiden would never enter her home as history with its wagons of sorrow stood between her and the new day.

Menachem returned to the suburb of Bet-Zetha. The camels still lay in front of his father's house. As he entered the house he noticed servants, a couple of Kushites and an Ethiopian moving the furniture outside. There was a hustle and bustle in the house. Just like fever precedes death, much activity occurs in a house soon to be abandoned. Swiftly Menachem entered the rooms in front of the tank where the rain water was caught. In the center of one of the rooms stood his father. Marcus Mercator was a tall, stout man. He wore a neatly trimmed, glossy beard. The merchant had a massive stomach bulging under his red cloak. As always a hearty smile adorned his lips as though he had invited the whole world to partake of a feast. He, in any event, was ready for the feast.

Menachem went up to him. Marcus took both his hands and kissed him on the cheeks. "You already know, my son, that we are leaving today. We are moving to Damascus. You will be welcome there too."

"Father," Menachem asked, "why do you flee in the hour of danger?"

"To save our hearth and home, my son. Our land is no longer safe, here we are going through difficult times—when the sea turns stormy and there is a port nearby, the captain who does not seek refuge there is a fool and a criminal."

"Ought the people not be saved, father?"

"I can only save myself, son. I do what I can."

"Then you do not believe that there is a way out for Israel?"

"That I know not but for an Israelite of means and good repute there is always a way out."

"Outside the land, is it not?"

"Outside the land."

"And away from the people, is it not?"

"And away from the people."

"You must leave forthwith, father. Sometimes the door of destiny closes before an individual can escape."

"A wise man foresees that. There is still time. We must leave here in any case. It has become dangerous in the land of Israel."

"Not only is there danger here in Israel, father, there is danger in all mankind."

"If I save myself, my young wife and our wealth before the Romans burn down everything here as punishment for the criminal rebels, I would have saved something."

"Do you take Israel with you to Damascus?"

"I take Chava and our gold with me, my son."

"One can take Israel along to Syria too, but you do it not," observed Menachem.

"I am taking our means. Later you will thank me for it."

Menachem smiled because his father gave him such a benevolent and amicable look.

"Come to me sooner or later, Menachem. You know how dear you are to me. May God be with you!"

"If I come, father, I shall bring Israel with me. What if it is even more dangerous there than here?"

"Bring whom you will.

You think and speak in riddles. You inherited that from your mother. Even so, I am pleased to hear it.

You are my child and everything about you is dear to me.

Come son, let me bless you."

Menachem bowed his head and received his father's blessing. Then he swiftly crossed the veranda to his mother's room, still smiling at the ease with which his father had found a solution to the secret that the future holds.

BOOK TWO

The Trials

1

WITH FIRMS STEPS YESHUA hastened towards the desert of Judea. He had forsaken his father's house because he found life insufferable. In his heart he felt that he must shed light on something but he knew neither what nor how he must do it. And too great a burden could suffocate anyone and make them pine away. A new way had to be found to relieve the pressure of the times. But where was this road to be found? Yeshua could not conceive that Ben Nesher had expected deliverance from the path of the Zealots. He doubted the way of the Pharisees. Was it necessary to create a new rule as a commandment?

The Torah is an everlasting tree. God gave it to the people of Israel once and for all. It always bears fruit. It loses no fruit even though many may eat of it. Why do people come there to graft branches—human branches—on the boughs of the Torah? The Pharisees are stupid people. They know not the difference between the olive tree which grows new branches, which bears fruit and loses them again, and the eternal tree of the Torah which cannot grow and which cannot lose fruit, no matter how many may feed on it. The way of the Revelation had to be new for the burden upon the breast of the people was heavy.

Yeshua's feet trod vigorously on the stony road. Heavy was his hair, black and mingled with chestnut brown. Now it was whipped by the wind and now it fell back upon his neck like a spent wave.

And Yeshua walked on; a strong wind seemed to accompany him. Over his head passed flocks of great birds that came from the sea. At this moment he had power and life with him even as he had the wind behind him.

When he became hungry he turned into a side-road for he was in no haste of coming late and because side-roads are just as good as the main road.

The side-path into which Yeshua had turned emerged upon a small quadrangular plateau where a wretched hut stood which belonged to two old people. Around the hut a couple of goats grazed in the scanty vegetation. Before Yeshua entered he cast a glance at the mountainous country which enclosed the plateau on all sides. Grim grey rocks and pink slopes rose and fell as far as the horizon. On the other side the blue sea rolled in the distance. And after Yeshua had saluted the landscape he entered the cottage. He found an old man and woman seated upon a couple of stones, upon which the woman ground her meal.

"Baruch ha-ba," said the old man: "'Blessed be he that comes.' When one is so alone like we are, stranger, the one who visits is like a beam of light in the darkness."

"Man has need of man," answered Yeshua, "but he treats him falsely."

"We had five children. Two left us and three were taken away by the Romans. We never heard from them again. I think they are dead. We survive them, but in the wrong life."

"There is only one life," said Yeshua.

"Believe you not then in the Olam ha-ba, the world to come, young man?"

"There is only one life. If there are two halls with an open door in the middle, do the rooms form a house or not?"

"You speak well, young man. You know more than we. Look, that is the only one here who still grows above the ground, a grandchild, the little daughter of Penina."

In front of the door of the mud hut stood a girl.

"Her name is Chedvah," said the old man.

"I am weary," said Yeshua. "I have walked for twelve hours. I come from Galilee."

"Go lie down there in the corner, there's a mat. Our house is small. There is nothing except for the space where we sit. We shall stay awake so that you may rest."

"At night the lamp must remain burning. This young man is a light, a light in Israel, see you not?" the woman told her husband. Let them sleep and burn. Verily we shall stay awake, thus we will do no harm."

The small girl Chedvah was curious. She bent over Yeshua, fascinated by the beauty of the young man; he was of the age which she aspired to.

Yeshua fell asleep quickly and quietly and in his sleep he took his hosts along with him. Now he walked up and down the tired old roof of the dwelling which was so moldy that it contained holes here and there through which one could look down. He cast his glance over the horizon. Mountains loomed up threateningly and the great sea stretched out like an infinite blue cloak on which people and souls might gently glide away. Looking up, he whispered, "The Father is everywhere." Then all of a sudden he had to look down through one of the holes in the roof.

He saw the two old people staring with bent backs at the ground at Chedvah, the little daughter of their child that was lying on a small mat. Her face was flushed with fever while her tiny tongue brushed across her dry lips. "She is the only one of us who still grows above the ground," the old people had said. Old Amitai had thought the same when he leaped like an ape to the breast of his son. The Romans had let the old man die, rolling him down the mountain slope. Chedvah shivered with fever. Yeshua saw the helplessness of the two old people. They did not even clearly comprehend this misfortune that had once more come knocking at their door. They were too close to their dotage to be able to help a child.

They looked down and saw her slowly dying, and with her the light in themselves was going out. But they could not make anything better.

It was then that Yeshua's heart melted at last. Too much had accumulated there—the grief of the people had become so dense that his heart had turned to stone. Now, it was not only the suffering of the dying child that stirred his compassion.

All the suffering that he had witnessed suddenly softened in his breast. He descended to join them in the room at the feet of the child with the old man at her left and his wife at her right. A strange feeling took hold of him. His breast burst open, his eyes popped, he became like a tree that brought forth buds in an instant. He felt his blessing extending to the child like a ray of light as he mumbled some words that he had meant to say earlier or intended to say later. "Talitha kumi,"—stand up, child—he said in the soft Aramaic speech. The child, whose head appeared to be burning with fever, abruptly turned white and arose with her arms extended towards him.

The change in the appearance of the two old people was even more dramatic. They raised their arms halfway whilst their faces, helpless from despair just a moment before, turned radiant with joy. A miracle had taken place. How great it was to perform a miracle! "Whoever could do that must be beloved by the Lord," thought Yeshua. But he did not know whether he still had time to bethink himself of this. The tree closed all its buds once more. The sorrow was locked in his breast again. Then he departed while thinking, "what purpose does all this serve?" He felt no more pity for the poor people and Chedvah.

He did not even think of them anymore. There were thousands of old people and many Chedvahs. If all felt salvation came from God, more might be won. And if all felt that he came from God then perhaps it might be easier to bring redemption and take them to the Father. Was it true what he had said that morning—that a house consists of only two rooms and that the door between is open? If the door, however, is unlocked then the watchman still calls upon the leader to open it. Should the gate be closed or only be opened a little, then a watchman is needed to open it. Think you still, Yeshua, that the track of angels is so light upon the earth? Let no such thoughts cross your mind for they are effaced before you have followed them.

It was night when Yeshua quit the hut at the crossroads.

2

NATURE ITSELF GENERATED HEAT. The red earth glowed. The trees stood motionless in the grip of the azure sky and the flowers were already withered, drooping like brown threads on the plant which had produced them. Yet the people were drawn up in vast numbers at the town of Beth Abara where preached Yochanan, the prophet of repentance.

A great multitude had gathered there. Bedouins from the deserts of Perea and Idumea and men both notable and humble from the great cities. Feeling themselves burdened down by the times, the people sought relief in salvation.

Yochanan the Baptist was a tall, rough peasant with a wild, twisted growth of beard. He wore a prophet's cloak of undyed camel's hair which gave him a shaggy and primitive appearance, like an animal that lives on the red soil of the banks of the Jordan. Around his loins was a girdle, perchance to show that his belly was unclean and still belonged completely to the kingdom of the beasts. Yochanan did not preach from love of people. He hated them since he knew they were hypocrites. Of the thirty who had suffered him to wash away their sins, at best only one deserved it. He demanded much but had not God commanded it to be written down, "You will be a people of priests to me?" In that mark of devotion lay too heavy a duty. It was the obligation by which the prophets demanded too much from the nation. A group of priests and their supporters belonging to the Sadducee party had arrived at Beth Abara in their beautiful garments on horses and in carts. Wavering between respect and unwillingness, the poor folk made way for them. Now they stood before the Baptist. Yochanan remained silent. More simply clad Pharisees refused to be crowded out by the Sadducees. They wore tzitzit prayer threads in the hem of their outer vestments and felt secure in their attire with their thick black beards and earnest eyes.

When Yochanan had the group of Pharisees on the right and the Sadducees on the left, he abruptly opened his mouth and began to curse them.

"Viper's brood!" he shouted, dismissing them with a gesture of his hand. "Who told you that you could escape God's wrath which breaks loose like a tempest? Where are the fruits that show me you have truly repented of your sins? Comfort yourselves not with the thought that you are descendants of Abraham, for I say to you that God can raise children of Abraham from the stones of the road."

Menachem, who had moved closer, abandoned the multitude into the center of which he had been pushed, in the hope of approaching Yochanan. Although he wished to see and hear the prophet, he felt no need for baptism.

Presently he found a place on the banks of the Jordan between the tall rushes from which new stalks shot out as the old ones withered, drooping down like rusty swords. He watched the company of prim, shamefaced Sadducees. They shrugged their shoulders, smiled contemptuously but were afraid nevertheless. They departed without looking back. The Pharisees did not withdraw; they had taken Yochanan's harsh words to heart and gestured violently. Menachem pitied them. The aristocratic lords who had likewise come to speak about Yochanan did not soften him, however. For verily, Pharisees were so little hypocrites that they did not at first understand what Yochanan meant. These people did their best for God; now they were being chased away like black sheep. Yochanan cried to them that on the Day of Judgment the chaff would be separated from the wheat. The Pharisees thought that by chaff he meant them, so they arose indignantly. Nevertheless they were accustomed to being chastised by God's words and by men of God. Some stared at the ground in despair.

"Let us depart from here, we do not belong here, we are not wanted!" exclaimed one of them bitterly. Menachem felt sorry for them—on his mother's side he stemmed from a family of scribes. He knew the history of his people, what sufferings his ancestors had endured to bring forth these men who were so devoted to the Law! They were his forefathers' good intentions made flesh and blood. Now they had been summarily rebuked and dismissed. How humbly they stood there, the faithful heirs who had not squandered their inheritance like all the generations of Israel before the Exile whom the prophets had reviled like Yochanan had now done to the Pharisees. It was rumored amongst the people that Elijah the Danite had returned in Yochanan the Baptist in order to rouse Israel before the Great Day arrived.

The crowd opened again. A man had arrived in Beth Abara after a day's journey of eight hours. Power and authority radiated from the newcomer, for each stepped aside so that he was able to draw near to the Baptist as though guided by faith.

Menachem's eyes opened wide and a cry of exultation burst from his throat.

"Yeshua!" He had recognized his friend. "Now everything will be all right," he thought. "We are saved." His trust in Yeshua had never been as great as when he saw him at that moment.

Yeshua had now reached the presence of the Baptist. Yochanan, whose body seemed to experience sudden jerks as though violent emotions and wild words pressed against him like young eagles in their mountain nest, had regained his ideal composure. He stood tall and erect, eyes shining brightly and arms raised. "Come, my master," he exclaimed. And the people began to rejoice as though two famous warriors who had won great victories for them had finally joined forces.

Yeshua and Yochanan seemed to have a conversation but they were so far away that Menachem could not hear their words. Later he heard that Yochanan had called Yeshua "God's own son." This was possible for before Yeshua had thrown off his coat and plunged into the Jordan, the Baptist had bowed low before him. Menachem had seen that with his own eyes. And also many strange things were heard later concerning the baptism of his friend Yeshua in the Jordan. People said that when Yeshua returned to the bank, a bird had settled upon his shoulder and this bird represented the Shechinah, the embodiment of God's splendor, which the people started calling the "Ruach haKodesh," the Holy Spirit, from that time forth.

Menachem who had known Yeshua as a youth in Nazareth recognized that he was not in a position to add anything to or detract anything from their admiration and goodwill towards his friend.

He headed towards Yeshua who had emerged from the Jordan and called his name. Yeshua looked him in the eye, spoke not a word of greeting but placed his hand on the shoulder of a man in the crowd, saying, "Follow me." Menachem recognized the man as a Galilean from Capernaum.

The night lay dark over the land of the Jordan, permitting no gleam of light but pushing down everything that possessed life and form. Thus it rendered the life of daylight non-existent. Night covered earth and nothing was itself anymore. Where were now the multitudes, the Baptist, the Pharisees and Sadducees?

Menachem was awake, however. He searched the banks of the river and the hills nearby until he found Yeshua by the light of a small torch which was immediately extinguished. Menachem concealed himself behind a rock which rose up like the horn of a mighty rhinoceros. Yeshua was standing in the middle of a group of men whom he had that day chosen. A few faces looked familiar to Menachem from his youth in Galilee. Why had Yeshua chosen mostly strangers and ignored him?

"I am leaving now but I shall return," he heard Yeshua tell the men around him. "None of you may follow me."

One of them asked him, "Before you leave us, master, tell us, is it true that you are the Messiah?"

"Truth resides not in a word," Yeshua replied. "Would that be the answer," wondered Menachem, "Messiah? May God grant it be so. I will follow him; I wish to reconcile with my friend."

Yeshua ascended the slope of one of the mountain chains leading away from the Jordan in a south-westerly direction. The air was oppressive and laden with doom. Nearby lay the Dead Sea with its hard metallic waves that resembled bears' paws. Yeshua sought not the sun as he proceeded towards the Judean desert.

"God has guided me towards the wilderness of humanity. God has directed me to wander amidst the sin and the sorrows. I know now what path He has in mind for me. Even if I have to pass through the flames of Gehennom, I am going in God's direction. That brings peace."

So he spoke as the desert encompassed him on all sides, "The Father has locked me up so that He may redeem me in the hour of His choosing." Then he turned around in the darkness and perceived the figure approaching him.

"Menachem, why do you follow me?" he asked abruptly.

Menachem clearly discerned the white figure of Yeshua in the boundless night.

"I follow you, my friend, as I cannot run beside you."

Their words remained hanging in the stillness as though they did not intend to fade. Then they strode on but although Menachem wished to follow Yeshua and Yeshua fancied that his friend still pursued him, they went their separate ways.

Yeshua headed for the desert hills while Menachem turned eastwards towards the forested valley of the Jordan.

"They have named me Messiah," thought Yeshua as he walked on in the cold night while the wind lifted up his garment like wings. "Am I the Messiah, Father? I wish to be him for in truth the measure is full and the people are miserable. Am I the Messiah? It must be so. How else would I be able to do something for the suffering people? I knew it not. I was a child and I played. I have seen the Temple and heard the Law being explained. I have seen the affliction of Israel and felt the iron hand of the Romans. And, my God, it is true, I cannot bear it any longer. I was no Messiah then. But my Father in heaven, you can make me a Messiah now—I am willing and obedient. You were with me at my birth and you know the hour that you made me Messiah. Your sponge has soaked up all the sorrow; squeeze it and let my blood become dew on the heads of the people."

Then Yeshua became silent and thought no more but walked deeper into the desert without hunger or thirst. It was still night.

3

WHEN WEARINESS OVERTOOK HIM he sat down on top of a hill amidst some rocks. The sun appeared on the horizon and rose swiftly and inexorably like a fiery eagle with innumerable wings that spread ever wider until they disappeared into the blue, leaving only the body of flames. He felt no hunger or thirst. He lowered his head to his arms that rested upon his knees. Then he sagged backwards and the back of his head came to rest against a sharp outcrop which pressed against the spot where the skull and the spinal column met. It was as if his head had risen into space, a skull over the Judean desert which burned obediently in the sun's tormenting rays.

In front of him appeared a tall man in a white robe that looked like a Bedouin from the land of Kedar. Lean like a rake, the man had yellowish grey sunken cheeks stubbed with beard. His skin resembled that of a roasted fowl. One eye was half closed while the other carried a mocking look and his mouth made a skew cut in his face. "What is this man's name?" wondered Yeshua. Suddenly the head leaned back and the mouth opened, audibly sucking in a draught of air, to speak as if he were spitting out the words:

"So you are the Messiah, Yeshua?"

"You say so."

"The messiah must fulfill many things, know you that?"

"I know it."

"How will you save mankind?"

"By blessing them."

"Is that enough, Yeshua?"

"By healing them."

"Is that enough, Yeshua?"

"I will bear their sorrows so they may rest."

"Is that enough, Yeshua?"

"I will pray for them, day and night."

"Will that suffice, Yeshua?"

"I shall bring them to the Father."

"Can you do that, Yeshua? There are some who are always with their Father and others who will never get there."

"Oh my God, if that is still not enough, I will give them my blood and die for them."

"Is that enough, Yeshua? What will they gain thereby? You will be dead. Your flesh will be devoured by vultures and jackals will drink your blood but the people will continue to suffer and their flesh too will be eaten by vultures and their blood lapped up by jackals."

"Be quiet! Close your accursed mouth. You are Satan himself. Now I recognize you. I shall go to my Father and entreat him: 'Raise the dead, choke the vultures that devour man's flesh and strangle the jackals that sip their blood! Give me the power, Father, to remove their sins even as You do away with death.'"

"Words, words, words, Yeshua. And good intentions. You cannot achieve anything worthwhile. Man cannot be of any use to man even though he rages against his own body."

"In the name of my Father who is in heaven, I command you to go away, Satan."

"Good, good, I shall depart, Yeshua. But I shall return frequently. Then will you curse me, asserting that I return unbidden, but in truth I shall never appear at the door of your soul unless you summon me, Messiah."

As the old Bedouin was disappearing, a new figure took his place.

It was a great man with a long full beard and eyes that discharged immense power, wrapped in a mantle of flaming yellow gold. It was as if all the pollen of the world radiated from his garment.

"Are you the Messiah?" he asked in a voice which was sweetly young, like that of a mother of twenty eight years.

"You say so, Master," Yeshua replied. "I have been waiting for you."

And Yeshua took care that he bowed the upper part of his body at the same time that the tall greybeard bowed.

"Moshe Rabbinu, Moses our teacher," murmured Yeshua softly and lovingly.

"Yeshua of Nazareth," said the ghost of Moses, "do you wish to be Messiah?"

"I wish it."

"Yeshua, I did not want to be a leader of Israel but I yielded for the sake of God. I loved this nation more than my heart. I slew an Egyptian because Egypt tried to break my people, even though I knew that God had commanded us not to kill. I was even willing to sin for the sake of Israel. I refused to become the leader of my people out of fear that I would fail in my love, for I loved them greatly. I could save them once but not forever, not after my death. Who can save a people forever, Yeshua? Is there upon the earth a Noah's ark wherein one can place a beloved people, rub one's hands and exclaim joyfully: 'Now are they safe forever!' I was their leader and after the old leader new leaders came. But think about it: Messiah is unique, he will do the work once and for all."

"Love you my people enough, Yeshua? I saw Israel's sins and did not run away from them after I had been with the Father. I returned to them and I begged God: Forgive them, they are only human; let them not fall if I find favor in Your eyes. For they are my brethren whom I love dearly and You have brought them still closer to my heart by suffering me to work for them, grieve for them and plead for them. They are my runaway children, they stumbled and they returned to me sick. Let me become old, my Father, so that I may work for them, for they are fallen and cannot walk far anymore, while their arms quickly get exhausted. Will you still be Israel's Messiah, Yeshua?"

"I wish to be Messiah for the sake of mankind."

"Wait!"

Moses' apparition disappeared and there came forth men, strangers, in the short, red, sleeveless attire of the Romans. They drove a bearded, thirty year old Semite before them. The Jew was accompanied by his little daughter who laid her hand upon the man's bound hands. When the group reached a pile of faggots they halted abruptly.

His tormentors removed the shackles from the Israelite and placed the girl next to the woodpile.

"Do you believe in God?" asked the captain of the guards. He wore a Roman helmet.

"Do you believe in God and in His help at this hour?"

"Do you believe your Messiah has come?"

"Nay, if the Messiah were here, these things would not happen."

"Is that your small daughter?"

"Aye."

"Set her upon the faggots."

The strangers placed the girl on the wood while they held her arms tightly. Yeshua passed a hand before his eyes for the child was exceedingly sweet and her large eyes were as serious as they were innocent. She reminded him of Chedvah whom he had saved in his vision and perhaps must save now. "Talitha kumi," he muttered and his heart pained him sorely. But the girl did not arise from the stake.

"I believe that he must come," replied the Israelite.

"Stubborn man, you refuse to believe! Kindle the faggots, men."

"Father, father, remain staunch!" called the child and in order to encourage him she raised both hands to heaven and reverently professed the unity of God.

The faggots, however, began to crackle and reached the feet of the girl like waves on the Sea of Kinnereth that tarry on the beach. Suddenly the Semite exclaimed, "Stop, put out the fire, extinguish it! God, who returned Isaac from the altar of sacrifice to the bosom of Abraham, does not wish it. Spare my child, strangers, and take me."

"Nay man, first shall you see your child burn and then you shall feel yourself how speedily fire changes a man's skin."

"I believe that my Messiah has come!" screamed the father.

"Extinguish the fire!"

"Hallelujah, hallelujah!" cried the strangers. "At last his eyes have been opened." Then they threw woolen blankets on the feet of the girl that were already burning.

The Jew turned to Yeshua and said: "Forgive me, Yeshua, I was ready to ascend the stake for the glorification of God's Holy Name but may I sacrifice my daughter for the sanctification of His name? Can one sacrifice another? Or am I merely weak and would rather perish myself than behold the death of my daughter? Why does God demand so much of a person?"

"Think of Abraham," said Yeshua. "But tell me, who are you?"

"The folk of Israel."

"I knew it."

Then raised Yeshua abruptly his arms to heaven and called out: "Oh Father, Father, this is my flesh which I give to people, this is my blood with which I shall redeem them, but place not my sister Rachel beside me on the sacrificial altar!" And he screamed, "away, begone Satan, you will not tempt me from the path that I must follow."

"Do you still wish to be Messiah now, Yeshua?" called the shrill voice of the Satanic Bedouin of a moment before.

"I want nothing. I only desire that my Father's will be done, Amen," cried Yeshua as though already all of Israel's torments had entered him.

"So you are doing it for me, my son?" asked a stately, slender woman clad in white. She had full breasts, barely veiled. Her features were soft as though the hands of grief and love had never left her.

"Who are you, woman?"

"Humanity."

"I knew it."

"My children are all sick but how fair they were when I brought them forth," sighed the woman. "Can you save them, Yeshua? Will you give them back to me, so sweet and pure and good and whole as they were in my eyes when I gave birth to them?"

Yeshua gazed at the apparition with love because there was so much love in the woman's eyes. Then he gently replied:

"Their grief for me and their sins shall pass through my fingers like the sands and disappear in the sea of God's limitless compassion."

"Wait a minute!" pealed the voice of the Bedouin. "Can you save them?"

The scene in front of the afflicted man became blank. Then appeared before Yeshua's eyes the old man Amitai. He sprang like an ape upon the breast of his tall son Barzilai. Did he do this in order to snatch his son away from the grip of the Romans or so that he could be with him? Old people sometimes acted strangely; they still wanted to protect their children whilst looking for protection too. The Romans had thrown the old man to the ground and although he had lived like a good Israelite and his heart was simple, his strength did not suffice. The Romans stepped on him and although he had still wanted to live and clung frantically to the stones, they kicked him into the abyss. Now he lay dead, like a shattered vessel.

"I wanted to die for the man!" cried Yeshua.

"You could have died for him, Yeshua, but one can only die once, and for one man only. What would it have served? Would your death have remedied any deed in the course of the centuries?"

"Silence, I can save his soul! The soul of the good old Amitai!"

"Let the souls save themselves, Yeshua. The door between the two rooms is still open, did you not say so yourself? Is not the Kingdom of God still available everywhere for those who carry it within themselves?"

"The door is closed. I shall reopen it," cried Yeshua.

"Aha, you seek a place and a reason for existence."

A screeching laugh followed.

"Oh my son, how great is your compassion!" resounded the ghostly voice of the figure in whom Yeshua had recognized humanity. "You are willing to die in order to help my children!"

"But he also knows that either no help exists or that help is already there, also without him. He is searching for a way in which to serve mankind. His pity seeks an outlet. He is willing to give up his life for them because he does not know how else he can help them!" shrieked the invisible Satan, and continued: "Yeshua, Yeshua, you hold your flesh and blood ready because you don't know any other means of redeeming the children of mankind. But will that avail? Can you be of use to them, you son of despair?"

Then the apparition of humanity resumed: "Yeshua is a child of hope. My children look to him."

"Nay, Yeshua is the child of despair!" shouted the shrill voice of Satan. "He is Israel's despair. Jesus ben Israel seeks an escape for his people and his compassion by drilling open a path to God."

"Silence, be still, Satan, and you, woman of humanity! You speak in difficult words about simple matters. I follow my Father's path. I know not who I am. But my Father shall proclaim who I am on the resting places of my journey."

And suddenly Yeshua found himself in a synagogue. A rabbi was preaching but the shrieks of a madman started interrupting him as he was discussing a chapter of the Law. Yeshua got up and touched the one who was possessed.

The madness left him and he exclaimed "Hallelujah" at the top of his voice.

"Why have you profaned the Sabbath?" the rabbi asked sternly. Yeshua shrugged his shoulders.

"Does God wish there to be one more hour of suffering upon the earth if one can end it?" he asked the rabbi.

Then disappeared the synagogue, the rabbi, the Jews and the madman although the voice of the demon made itself heard again:

"Yeshua, you have healed a madman but have you removed the curse of madness from all the insane to the end of time?"

"Silence, you have been sent by Satan," said Yeshua. He reflected a moment and mumbled, "in my Father's house the event outweighs the number. See where the lightning has struck a house. Does the beam burn only where it was struck? Behold, I cast a drop of oil upon the water. Does the drop float only where it fell? A dart breaks but a drop binds."

"Lovely words, Yeshua, but they do not silence the groans of those in pain nor do they make the dead child rise to comfort its father and mother."

"There is no death. My love for them has conquered it."

"I know it. You are full of good will, child of despair!"

"Child of hope!" cried humanity. Then Satan became silent and also the voice of humanity.

Yeshua considered where to betake himself. He sat there pensive, his head resting on his hands. Before him a scale was dangling where each saying was divided across two weights.

Suddenly, however, the figure of Menachem appeared.

"Who am I, my friend," Yeshua asked the companion of his youth.

"Surely you yourself know that," the image replied.

"Nevertheless my friend, I pray you to tell me."

"A way out for the Jews, a purpose for the other nations, Yeshua. Surely you know it!"

"I know it but we may both know only one part of what we are."

"That is so."

"God does not permit his envoy to execute all which the envoy would like to do. God created them together. He clove their souls in their appointed lot. In His purpose they remain bound and so they stand marked upon the plan."

Menachem turned away from Yeshua with a glance full of unfathomable longing and irrevocable decision.

Yeshua's thoughts deepened and became so dense that he thought: "Now am I shut out forever from them. My thought is surely as firm as the earth's crust and I have now made a hole which nothing from the external world can penetrate anymore . . ."

But again a new world opened before him and this time it was densely populated.

He stood in a white garment in the midst of an open plain. Burning hot shone the sun over infinite grass speckled with red, white and blue flowers. The sky was rolled out across the plain as though it not only stood above these strange meadows but sealed the edges of the plain, and also must reach below. In a tunnel of sparkling blue lay the ground on which Yeshua stood. On both sides of him a vast multitude had gathered, raising their arms to heaven.

"Give us a Messiah!" pleaded the people on the right in who Yeshua recognized his people Israel, "the time is ripe, we cannot wait any longer. We stand bursting like fruit in the autumn. If we fall on barren ground, the fruit of our longing will be lost and withered! Give us a Messiah for we are like a mother and can no longer keep the fruit in our womb."

It was exceedingly easy to recognize the people of Israel. All wore the white garments with sky blue stripes from their bridal gown with God's covenant.

The hordes of other people were more varied. There were countless Romans in tunics and sleeveless togas, Greeks in white festive garb, Germans in animal skins, Scythians and even black people from the land of Kush.

And all cried out: "Give us a God! Our gods are dead and have forsaken us! Give us a God, Yeshua. We want a welcome for the hour when we see our parents die. It is so needful, Yeshua, we are alone at the momentous hours of life and death, give us a God . . ."

Then the men lowered their arms and the women, Roman, Greek, German, Ethiopian and Nubian raised their arms, shouting, "Show us a man, Yeshua. Give our husbands and sons an idol! We have no God, and we know not man, even though we bear him children. The times are ripe, Yeshua, Jesus!" For they also called Yeshua "Jesus" in the manner of the Greeks.

Yeshua groaned and shook his head. Yet did he stretch out his arms to the crowds of Israelites and idolators.

A slender man stepped out in front of the army of Jews and stood beside Yeshua.

"Show us our Messiah. We have suffered overmuch. Slaves we were in Egypt and we wept for our lost holiness in Babylon. Day and night we wrestled with our own people under the guidance of our Prophets and against our own soul during our life upon earth for the glorification of His Name. Perhaps we do not walk in good order in God's way but we walk no more off the road. All nations have been over us and oppressed us. Egyptians and Philistines, Babylonians and Persians, Medes, Greeks and Romans. They tortured our body and we sanctified our heart. They kicked us in the belly but we laid our hands upon our heart and in our heart stood His Name. The Romans tried to wrest us away from God. Our hands are so tired, Yeshua. Show us Messiah, help us. The world is a bowl of injustice and the beaker is full. Empty it and fill it with God's justice. Those who wish to slay and defile us will surely ebb away from this land and from this people, like the sea recedes from the beach. But like a flood of prayers they will return to humble themselves before God and bear witness to His uprightness. Then will the Law go out from Zion and God's Word from Jerusalem. We have been waiting for You, Messiah, we are weary and eager."

"We demand more!" clamored the others. "A Messiah is not enough for us! We have no God. Give us a God!"

"Sanctify our sons," moaned the women, "so that our daughters can love man after the example of God."

Yeshua stood irresolute in the midst of the great multitude to the right and left of him. He understood their lamentations and desires and held both arms outstretched although he too was weary for he loved them both and wished to hear both for the sake of Heaven.

Then he sighed, lowered his arms and whispered, "let my Father's will be done."

Afterwards was Yeshua brought back to the world of sunlight. He felt a pain in the back of his head for he had rested it upon a sharp rock.

He stood up, stretched his arms, stirred his legs, shrugged his shoulders once more and muttered:

"I am willing to live for them, Father, and I am ready to die for them. Is it given for anyone to do more? If it be true that You have cursed man with the curse that he cannot help humanity, I beseech you, Father, for godlike strength for I am ready to become God for them. I entreat You humbly: make me mighty."

Yeshua raised his face heavenward. There were tears in his eyes.

"Your lot is cast, follow Yourself and you follow me," resounded a voice, and with calm steps which the savage regions where he had tarried did not know, Yeshua strode through the desert of Judea in the direction of the Jordan.

4

MENACHEM THOUGHT HE STILL followed Yeshua. He saw the white figure of his friend moving ahead of him in the distance despite the blackness of the night. The night was exceedingly dark and filled with the sounds of animals and other living creatures. People call these ominous noises. The noises, however, were rather the voice of sorrow, a yearning for something that could never be fulfilled. Sometimes the jackals barked for long periods in a choir of frenzied howls, as if one tried to show the others that its grief was greater than that of the others. Even the movement of boulders that strove to free themselves was evidence of the restlessness of matter. Immobility offered no repose so it was sought in movement.

Menachem continued on until he had lost the reassuring uniformity of the desert and dragon like contours of the mountains. He unexpectedly found himself in a forest without knowing how he got there.

"I have followed Yeshua because we belong together. Where is he now?" He had been removed from Yeshua's world and set down somewhere else.

"From their rustling leaves I know that I am surrounded by cedars and sycamores. There are also ferns that rub against my feet. I shall rest here tonight as sleep has already started to invade my thoughts."

"I am in God's hands; should it be his purpose that I be devoured by animals tonight, this will be done for tonight as I have neither the power nor the will to take precautions or to resist. Yet the night may even return me to Yeshua and the unavoidable path he has chosen."

Then Menachem fell asleep without noticing that he had laid down his head on thistles. He saw himself at the head of a long procession of camels, seated on a richly adorned carpet-saddle on top of a one-humped racing camel and beside him, fair as the nations and unveiled in Greek fashion, rode Yocheved with Jewish eyes and Jewish mouth. Behind them were the mounted and laden camels, so numerous that it was difficult to count them.

"Tomorrow you will become my husband forever," she said.

Jesus and Menachem

"Already Damascus is approaching where many tidings await us and where whole worlds may sink into oblivion. I'm proud, Menachem, that I ride beside you at the head of this bridal procession. They wish to make you king in Damascus which is filled with massive palaces and imposing temples. We will exchange a past of sorrows for a future filled with promise.

Look at the infinite sea that lies before us and not at the convulsed mountains behind us.

We have no more debts and no claims; that is my dowry to you."

The sun turned the universe into a temple of light when Menachem and Yocheved entered the city of Damascus.

Menachem's father, Marcus Mercator, came forward to meet them and called out:

"Come my children! My joy is complete today. My servants have prepared a feast."

They entered a synagogue where the marriage canopy had been erected and where Menachem beside Yocheved realized just how dear this woman was to him. A priest blessed their marriage after which father Marcus Mercator's face lit up with a fatuous smile of contentment—he believed that people have the ability to seal their own happiness forever.

Just as Menachem was about to slip the ring on Yocheved's finger a group of men with long beards and dark, deep-seated eyes burst into the synagogue with such violence that some of them stumbled over the hems of their garments.

"The hour is not yet come," they clamored.

"No wedding, no feast, Jerusalem is going up in flames!"

"We are here in Damascus," remarked Marcus Mercator. "The feast goes on; we have to think of ourselves too."

Menachem dropped his outstretched hand. Yocheved stared at him in disbelief and as he was casting off his splendid wedding garb, Menachem exclaimed:

"I am returning to my afflicted people in Jerusalem!"

"Why does one beget children and raise them in love?" exclaimed Marcus Mercator. "It matters not how sensible the parents are if the children prefer the flames of madness! Woe is me!"

"Can you save Jerusalem?" Yocheved softly asked Menachem

"I know not."

"But me you can save."

All of a sudden Yeshua appeared next to Yocheved under the marriage canopy. He gently touched her shoulder.

"There still remains much to be saved, Menachem. You can save your soul" said Yeshua.

"My soul is not as dear to me as Israel, Yeshua. The people that burn in Jerusalem weigh heavily upon my heart."

"What is a people, Menachem?"asked Yeshua.

"When suffering misfortune, a nation is a mother, Yeshua. Let me go now. There may yet be friends of mine that have escaped the flames, I need to be with them. Forgive me, Yocheved, for leaving you alone. Forgive me Yeshua for not putting my soul first; the one who thinks of his soul at this time lacks love."

"You are the one without love, Menachem. Yeshua thinks of the abandoned bride—you don't," Yocheved replied ruefully.

"I am only one man, Yocheved and Yeshua knows all about the anguish of having to divide one's devotion. The one demands so much whilst the others are so numerous. Accursed be those that avoid the death of their mother; let me therefore go with these men. Forgive me, Yocheved, Forgive me, Yeshua."

As the figures of Yocheved and Yeshua were dissolving, Menachem beheld himself accompanying the messengers from Jerusalem until he reached the city. His heart stopped beating as he watched her going up in flames as so many prophets had foretold. "Woe is me that my eyes behold what I feared."

The Temple was in flames; the holy of holies, the earthly abode of God. Menachem was unable to enter the burning city since vast crowds of pious people were fleeing the flames in the direction of the sea. Menachem knew instinctively that these people were not running at a natural pace. They were being driven. He saw nothing but feet, swiftly running feet, left feet attempting to escape the right and right feet striving to outpace the left. Beards blowing in the wind, measuring time by their movement. Gasping for breath, his hair billowing in the wind, Menachem raced after the Pharisees when Yeshua suddenly appeared in his path. He was wearing a white garment with a golden girdle around the middle, magnificent to behold.

"Why do you run, Menachem?" he asked in a friendly tone. "Do you also belong to the Pharisees?"

"Nay Yeshua, I belong not to the Pharisees yet I choose to remain with them."

"Why? Because they bear the scrolls of the Law with them?"

"Nay, Yeshua."

"Why then? Because they produce rules like bees produce wax? They build cells like the bee and dams like the beaver; God's burning wind destroys the cells whilst His rushing rivers wash away the dams."

"Although they are ignorant of what it is, they take something along with them, Yeshua. God has entrusted it to their hearts without their knowledge. It may well need to abide with them for a long time."

"What is it?"

"Israel's life!"

"They are running away in vain and from nothing. They can find it easily should they come to a halt, those refugees who flee from the consuming flames towards the crashing waves of the great sea."

"What do you speak of, Yeshua?"

"The Kingdom of God that they can find within. For that they do not need to flee from the leaping flames towards the crashing waves. I tell you in truth, Menachem, the Kingdom is not of this earth."

"So be it, Yeshua, but what we cannot believe exists not."

"The Kingdom of God is within us, Menachem."

"So it is but we must believe that we can establish it around us in order to maintain it within us."

"The people have strayed too much Menachem, I will give them rest."

"Rest Yeshua? Rest only arrives when one is taken away."

"And if we were lifted up, Menachem?"

Menachem found himself amongst the fleeing multitudes, running next to a tall man with a fluttering white beard who seemed to be a leader. His eyes rolled wildly in their sockets, the prayer shawl over his shoulders bat up and down like the wings of a pelican. He bore the scrolls of the law but he did not know that which he really carried: the invisible womb which gives birth to history.

"Where will we go?" Menachem asked him.

"We will be scattered amongst the nations as it is written in the Prophets."

Afterwards Menachem approached a strange city, weary and dusty. Beside him walked Yocheved, her back was bowed and her feet were large and flat. Between them a little girl, the color of her skin grey like slate. The three were sorely tired and they rejoiced when they finally saw a city that was inhabited. When they reached the first streets they encountered men and women outside their dwellings. As they approached Menachem walked up to a man who sat beside his wife in front of his house.

"What do you want?" asked the man

"I wish to live here," replied Menachem.

"What are you?"

"Jews."

"Oh you are Jews. Petrus, Marcus, Julius, Sabina, Vitellus, come here. There you have now Jews, those people of whom our priests have told us so much evil. Do you know what they have asked me? They wish to live here! Where shall we house them?"

"In the pig sty, Arminius! There the dung lies three thumbs high and they can sleep there warm and peacefully."

"And think of their sins," said a priest, approaching closer.

"They know already who we are and how they must deal with us before they have seen us. Our fame goes before us," remarked Menachem. "Come Yocheved, we are weary, we must stay with them. Perhaps they will become accustomed to our contact."

"Father, that child struck me!" cried Menachem's little daughter, gasping. The girl had stepped up to a low, lank-haired daughter of the inhabitants who was chewing bread; she had eyed the bread which the tall daughter of the inhabitants was calmly consuming but had not asked for any. Her eyes, however, had been bold. Slowly the tall girl arose. Chedvah, for so Menachem's child was named, had smiled thinking that now she would get some bread but instead she received a hard slap on her nose and mouth. When Yocheved saw her weeping child, she shrieked:

"We must go away from here, they already know too much about us, too much of what they wish to know. I cannot look upon the blood on my daughter's face."

"We must remain here, Yocheved."

"Why?"

"Because we must rest at the stopping places that are shown to us. The child, indeed, has no more strength to walk further."

"Let us rather go out into the night and die upon the stones."

"Nay, Yocheved, we may not die."

"Why may we not do that also?"

"Because we carry Israel's life with us!"

"Israel, always Israel. What does it do for us?"

But when the morning came Menachem regretted that he had remained in the town, hoping that the populace would become accustomed to strangers against whom they were incited by the priests. In the morning there came soldiers that chained them and brought them to a mountain. When they reached the summit, Menachem and Yocheved had to stand on the outermost edge of the precipice, flanked by two soldiers. Then came the colonels of the city, followed by two rows of soldiers that carried a wooden float on which Chedvah their daughter lay. When the procession reached the top of the mountain, the commanders called out:

"Now must you look closely and think of your sins."

"The soldiers picked up Chedvah, the daughter of Menachem and Yocheved; she was bound and could not defend herself but her eyes were wide open and mortally afraid for she had to enter death while still living.

"One, two, three, heave high, lads!"

Before the eyes of her parents they flung her into the abyss.

"Long live Israel, nonetheless!" gloated the men.

But neither Yocheved nor Menachem heard them for they had fainted away when their daughter had been hurled below. Losing consciousness is a divine mercy. The people found this grace, however, much too good for the two and they pricked them with lances in the thigh to restore them to consciousness.

Menachem opened his eyes.

"So Jew—and will you still always remain with Israel? God is so good to you, is He not?"

"Begone, Satan!" cried Menachem. "For the sake of the last link of the dead, for the sake of my daughter whom you murdered, I shall not break the chain. It leads to life."

But Yocheved who had also regained consciousness cried out: "Long live the murderers of children. By them is the right, the wisdom and the faith. Israel is Moloch and devours its own children. Woe be to our women!"

"Will you still remain by Israel? Will you still remain by Israel? Will you still remain by Israel?" thundered thousands of voices of creatures that circled Menachem's sleeping place in a mystic chain, a process that lasted a long time for the same people marched past him many times. First approached women of his tribe who gazed upon Yocheved and her mother Batsheba; they were followed by high-spirited Semitic women as the Egyptians had painted them, with curved nose, haughty eyebrows, high full breasts and strong hips.

"Will you still remain by Israel?" they taunted. "Will you still remain by Israel?"

All the other women asked him that now; humble, shabby women with rent petticoats and grimy feet. The eyes of some were closed. Trachoma ravaged their eyelids. After that the rows of mothers filed past Menachem. "Will you still remain by Israel?" cried the mothers in Israel who stared straight ahead. All of them bore a dead child in their arms and looked beyond it as though the creature in their arms were made of wood and still lived somewhere in the distance. The procession seemed to end for a while.

But then groups approached again. There followed men in Roman dress, men in Greek vestments, men in the garb of the Indian Ocean, and they said: "We have chosen, we do not belong there anymore. Will you still remain by Israel and see your wife plunged into misfortune and behold your children afflicted and tortured? Will you still remain by Israel at the expense of your flesh and blood?"

"Does my friend Yeshua consider himself and Miriam his mother?" replied Menachem. "Why should I think of the children of my flesh?"

Another throng of Jews followed. They were dressed in robes of mourning; they lifted the scrolls of the Law in the air and they had prayer thongs about their arms. However, they also wore blinders before their eyes and stoppers in their ears.

"My friends, why do you cover your eyes and ears?" asked Menachem.

"Not from the loss of our eyes and ears that God has created well but so that something will be shown to us, and we may be blessed," cried the Jews. "Good comes only from within and evil from without."

Then they demanded imploringly:

"Will you still remain by Israel, Menachem?"

The people who had turned around to ask him whether he wished to remain with Israel had suspended their mournful journey.

Suddenly Menachem stood in an immeasurable field overlaid with cut ears of grain braided together, offering the sun an unending bed for its rays. And there stood Yeshua again full of glory, enveloped in a white garment which was held firmly in the middle by a golden girdle. The people crowding behind Yeshua were innumerable, countless like the stars in heaven and the sands in the sea. There were great crowds of young women wearing blue veils. They gazed with love at the stern son of Nazareth.

But there were also countless men in cowls of prickly camel hair like Yochanan the Baptist wore. Despite gravity and age, they looked at Yeshua with a glance of adoration. And what Menachem found most beautiful— thousands and tens of thousands of children swarming like butterflies in a field of flowers, already playing around and between the men and women. They were playing quietly and peacefully directly in front of Yeshua.

On the other side were ranged the men dressed in garments of mourning. There were old men with white beards among them, but there were likewise men in the full prime of their years, whose beard was still black, and young boys with small black skull-caps. The women were bowed and heavily veiled. Those who were still fair of face or figure did their best not to be perceived. Here and there a scroll of the Law projected high above the multitude. Although they also stood on the open field under the sun and rested their feet on the ears of grain, the men and youths in the rear of the crowd were busy gathering up the ears of grain and braiding a sort of fence from the straw.

The millions and millions of men and women and even the tiny children who stood behind Yeshua now began to clamor too.

"Will you still remain by Israel, Menachem?"

Then shouted also the men of Israel, even those who were busy plaiting the wall, and the black-veiled women, those who had no more beauty, and those who avoided their own fairness.

"Will you still remain by Israel, Menachem?"

There was something so entreating and incredible in their voices, that Menachem was moved. And all at once there was a man full of glory between Menachem and Yeshua, and he said:

"Menachem, you were with me when I slew the Egyptian out of love for a depraved people!"

"Then is that already enough reason why I should stay with them!" cried Menachem.

And Moses continued: "Menachem, you were there nearby when I climbed Mount Sinai for their sake and received God into my frail earthly heart."

"Then is that sufficient reason for me to remain with them," repeated Menachem.

Moses disappeared and a young man in a short white tunic with naked legs and disheveled hair and a lyre in his hand stood before Menachem.

"Menachem, you were there close by when this host of gloomy people danced in joy to the sounds of my harp. Then they wore bright colors and the women's backs were unbowed and their hair uncovered. It was a joyous feast and the psalms streamed forth from me like water from a fountain. You were with us in the hour of joy, ages and ages past."

"Then is that enough reason for me to remain with them eternally, David my king," said Menachem, and he looked at the mourning people of Israel who waited fearfully for his answer.

Then Menachem turned to Yeshua:

"Yeshua, why do you not ask whether I will remain with Israel?"

"Because I know my Father's will, Menachem."

"Yeshua, Yeshua, tell me truly, can you give this people rest without removing them from the living? Then shall I stand beside you in the sun, for I am only a human being."

"In truth, Menachem, I cannot. It is not my Father's will."

"Do you still remain by Israel, Menachem?" shouted again the countless multitudes behind Yeshua.

"Do you still remain by Israel?" the Israelites, who were already half encircled by the hedge which their rear guard had twisted from the ears of grain, entreated sadly and disbelievingly.

"Menachem remains by Israel," said Yeshua then softly yet audibly to all. "For he is my comrade on the scale."

"I stand with Israel," repeated Menachem and he looked at Yeshua, "for I know that we are equals on the scale because our Father willed it so at the hour of His Creation."

Then did the image of Yeshua and of the countless other people fade from Menachem's vision. He still lay stretched out on the floor of the forest, his head on the thistles. Afterwards he dreamed that a wild beast had bent over him and that its teeth could have struck his neck. But the beast did him no harm and Menachem thought:

"Surely it is not God's will that the beast should slay me. Now I return to Israel."

Then he awoke and saw a young lion which must have passed exceedingly close to him, leaping away amongst the tree trunks. He brought a hand to his neck and it was wet from the saliva of the beast.

"Come, I am turning back to the banks of the Jordan!" he said to himself. He arose and in a few minutes reached the edge of the forest although he had been under the impression that he had penetrated it deeply.

He now had the yellow desert under his feet again and to his amazement he saw, only a hundred meters away, his friend Yeshua whom he had followed and lost from view, also heading in the direction of the Jordan.

BOOK THREE

The Unbidden Follower

1

YESHUA AND HIS FRIENDS were moving north towards Galilee. Far behind but close enough not to lose sight of them followed Menachem, the unbidden follower. He wished to learn the course his friend was taking and whether it was a good thing for Israel. He was moved when, on the banks of the Jordan, Yeshua with his hands on the shoulders of his friends had once again undergone the baptism that John the Baptist administered to sinners and doubters. Menachem envied Simon, Andrew and Yochanan whom Yeshua had chosen as companions. He was sorrowful that he, Yeshua's best childhood friend from Nazareth, was rejected. But he knew as well as Yeshua did that no pleading or imploring would change that. In these times, strange things were indeed happening with Menachem and Yeshua and the people of Israel.

After several days' journey, Yeshua and company reached the green Galilee where the earth shows her brighter side. Yeshua and his retinue had joined a vast multitude that had assembled on the shore of the large lake. Anemones and blue irises rose up through the grass; water flowed peacefully around the hairy reeds. The sky was so blue that one might well wonder how everything could remain within its embrace. Yeshua stood in the midst of what he called his "meshulachim," his apostles. From all sides he was called upon; the name Jesus resounded everywhere. That was how he had become known amongst the Greek speakers and in particular the many Greek Jews who followed him.

Menachem lay in the tall grass about one hundred meters from the edge of the crowd, propping his head on his hands, staring at Yeshua in the midst of the people. Then he got up and started to stride carefully towards the camp of the "Nazarenes" as the followers of Yeshua had become known in some circles. He had a sense of being observed, in the same way that he was observing the events. Under the clear sky no wind stirred the reeds along the shore, neither was there the semblance of a sigh in the branches of the tamarind trees and palms. Yet Menachem heard thunder in the distance, the noise of centuries of history and the sundering of bonds.

"*And I pray the mother stays alive and the child is born alive unto all eternity,*" he suddenly prayed. "*There are mothers that do not want to give birth yet they do. And there are daughters that blame the mother for not wishing to bear although they themselves do not want to bear, yet they do. Mothers must give birth and daughters cannot die.*" Menachem did not understand what these words meant that crossed his lips and had no time to reflect as something stirred in the group around Jesus. The men he called his apostles were moving in different directions, probably to obtain some food.

"Shall I go to Yeshua now? The time is right. But why should I attempt to achieve that which is doomed to failure? Has Yeshua ever properly looked me in the eye? He took me and placed me in front of him as if I were a glass of wine that he was sizing up. Yeshua never wanted to admit how much I cared for him. He saw our friendship as temporary. I often made it clear to him how much I cared by dropping pieces of my love at his feet where they shone like gemstones. I know he noticed but he never picked them up and I know he wants me to believe that he never noticed my affection. Maybe that is his duty. Maybe I myself must also deny many gifts?"

His musings were disturbed by a heavy grip on the shoulder. The grip spoke of someone who felt empathy for his neighbor but did not recognize his adulthood, the way that people deal with school children.

"Who are you?" the man firmly demanded. Recognizing one of Jesus's friends, he replied: "I am Menachem, son of Marcus Mercator from Nazareth."

"Who are you?"

"I am Simon who the Master calls Cephas, which means 'ha-eben,' the stone. But I'm not an 'eben ha-etser,' a stone of help, just a poor fisherman. The Master has remade me. I don't know any more what I used to be and nothing is left of Simon. The Master insists on the name Cephas although I don't know what he means by it."

"I know the Master, Simon. We have often had long conversations without using many words."

"Then you are not a Pharisee either."

"Perhaps I am reckoned with the Pharisees without belonging to them."

"Your words confuse me, a simple fisherman. You remind me of the Master. Are you related to him?"

"Nay, but we grew up together in Nazareth."

Suddenly Menachem thought of something:

"Simon."

"The name in Latin is Petrus . . ."

"Simon Petrus then . . . can you do something for me?"

"We are here to help one another, that is what the Master expects of us."

"Does Yeshua know that I am here?"

"He sent me to look for you, asking why you were always nearby and requested that we investigate."

"Tell him: out of love. And tell him: because for a while yet I have to follow the same route until our paths diverge. That is why I follow him, and, Simon Petrus, please ask the Master why I am not allowed in your midst. I know it cannot be, that it is not permitted. Still, perhaps he knows why I am not allowed to be with him."

"I shall ask him, stranger, but I do not expect anything good for you to come out of the reply. The Master has an open heart, almost anyone is welcome to approach him."

"All except the sinners who refuse to admit their sins and the Pharisees who think they do their duty."

"Exactly. Yet he welcomes almost everybody as he came to give and receive them in his heart. His heart is the grand feast hall of God in which a gift already awaits every guest. So if he has seen and not summoned you, I fear it does not bode well. As of now I'm still speaking with you and would wish you peace but if the Master calls you his enemy, then may you be damned. The enemy of my master is cursed by God."

"I am not your Master's foe, Simon. Please go and come back to tell me what the Master has against me."

"I will, but where will I find you to give you the answer?"

"Tonight I'll wait at this olive grove, Simon."

Evening came too quickly for Menachem as he would have preferred to postpone the separation between his friend and himself. Night settled heavily over the Sea of Kinnereth, over the hilly banks, the bushes, the valleys adorned with flowers of every color. The clear skies revealed the stars in their splendor which depressed Menachem even further as he contemplated their indifference. Everything is great for its own benefit and nothing is so great that it shares the sorrow and the joy of all. Menachem stood listening with his hand behind his ear. He resembled a hungry predator waiting restlessly to go on the prowl. Then he returned to his lair, waiting there on word from Jesus.

Loud footsteps announced the arrival of Simon Peter who was not a cautious man. He stopped to look around as he couldn't see Menachem anywhere. Menachem was well-disposed towards the huge, simple man chosen by Yeshua yet he outfoxed him as he had been creeping closer without the apostle noticing a thing. All of a sudden he stood up right in front of Peter, so close their clothes almost touched.

"Who are you, impostor?"

"No impostor, I am Menachem who has been waiting for Yeshua's word. Did you speak to him about me?"

"Aye, stranger."

"Did he say why I was not allowed to join his company?"

"He did say: 'That man does not believe in me.' I would have cursed you for that but Yeshua added: 'Yet we may not curse him.' Are you blind, man, you who spent so much time in his company, who grew up with him—not to believe in him?"

"Listen, Simon Peter, I may not believe what he wants me to believe. I still do not know what he wants me to believe but I care for him and it hurts me that he refuses to accept me in his circle as I want to know his way before I find mine."

"He is the will, the way and the word."

"That is possible!" Menachem replied.

"I have to restrain myself, stranger, not to kill you, as I have a knife with me. I won't, on his behalf. You are worse than the Pharisees."

"You would not serve Yeshua by killing me, Simon Peter. There will always be witnesses, whether one is killed or not."

"I don't like you, your tongue spews poison."

"Yet will I never betray your Master, Simon Peter. I do love him. But what does love mean to your Master? He wants faith. I have loved him since I was a child. He just let me go. He chose people for himself. Now he wants people to believe in him? I still believe in him but he will demand ever more faith as he proceeds along the path of his destiny."

"May God forgive you and bring you to your senses," shouted Simon Peter as he spun around in anger to return to Yeshua's camp.

2

THERE WOULD BE A marriage feast in Cana a few days later. By now Yeshua had become the star of Galilee. The youth and the women admired him. Only clear thinking Pharisees who were wary of his shears, those who were saddened to see further living leaves and branches fall from Israel, men who had already established their love and loyalty to Israel, spoke against Jesus of Nazareth. Much joy and acclaim surrounded him wherever he went; much surprise and zeal and the tinkling of silver bells because he brought a "besora tovah," a positive message. He had deservedly become the glory and the honor of the spring-land of Galilee so the people of Cana also welcomed him with open arms.

They made their way with sticks over their shoulders to which pouches were attached. Yeshua led the way, stick in hand, with the young Yochanan by his side, whose black locks undulated over his shoulders. There was the sturdy Simon Peter with his toughened hands, the man Nathaniel and the others who had all been chosen by Jesus. Far behind, with neither stick nor food for the road, followed Menachem, the unwanted follower.

In Cana, the wedding was turning into a massive feast. The nation chafed under oppression whilst foreboding clouded the future, thus people wanted to make the most of happy occasions like this. Wedding guests started arriving from towns like Capernaum, Magdala and Sepphoris. According to the custom of the area, Menachem squatted down on the wide court surrounded by sheep. One ewe chewed on his overcoat whilst her lamb placed its hooves on his knees. Chickens wandered about and over the men stretched out on the ground. A fountain of color decorated one corner of the square where women were holding conversation—their blue, red and yellow headscarves appeared to make up a single garment. Many discussed Yeshua who was going to attend and probably sit close to the bride and bridegroom, surrounded by his friends.

The women were talking of the miracles he had performed. One of them rose. She was tall and had lively eyes. "Blessed be Miriam," she said. "Blessed be the womb that bore him. He is Mosheach, can you not see?" A wave of awe and emotion swept through them. Even the men were quiet. Mosheach? Who can say if someone is God's Messiah? Only our children or grandchildren can make such a statement once the Messenger has long gone. People judge the Messiah by his works," one lean old man said when the moment of silence had passed. "He has performed many miracles," observed a young man. "Many have done that," the old man resumed. "The question is, can Jesus liberate Israel?"

From the women's side a voice simultaneously asked: "Can he make us happy?"

"I've heard it said," commented a middle aged fisherman, "that he can bring us to God after we have died."

"That is not necessary," said a third. "God comes to fetch us himself; He does not need any help." "No one knows what Mosheach will have to do, why he is coming and what he will be, maybe a king, maybe a beggar, maybe a warrior, perhaps a shepherd or a sage or even an uneducated man. No one knows why Mosheach is coming. One person thinks it is to heal his child, the other that he will come to free Israel from the Romans. A third thinks the reason is to do away with evil so that all of us may become Tzaddiks.[1]

Some are of the opinion that he will enable women to give birth without pain. Yet others claim that Mosheach will slay the angel of death and do away with mortality. Now there are even people with the opinion that Mosheach must bring us to God. Does God need help? But however it may be, if he comes to heal a sick child, that by itself would be enough."

"Dayenu—it would be enough for us!" the others exclaimed.

"Should he come to free Israel from the Romans, that would be enough for us!"

"Dayenu!" the others seconded.

"Should he come to remove evil from the world, that would be enough for us!"

"Dayenu!" the others agreed. And thus they proceeded in the familiar Eastern call-and-response manner, singing a litany of their people's

1. Righteous ones.

sorrows. They knew from long ago how sweet the healing from all that suffering, from all that evil, would be.

"Oh how deep and endless of hue this suffering is," thought Menachem. "If Yeshua is not the Messiah, he is willing to become one in order to relieve all that pain in one grand sweep. His heart is tender and behind his quiet, unmoving eyes he harbors much pain on account of all this suffering. If Yeshua is not the chosen son of God, he would want to become it in order to bear all the myriad sorrows of the people, of Israel and of the nations, and do away with it. He must have knelt and prayed: 'If I am not the Messiah, make me the Messiah in order to remove the pain. And if a Messiah cannot do it and only a God can help humanity, I am willing. Make me a God in order to do the work.'" He kept thinking along these lines: "Perhaps it is possible for God to turn someone into Mosheach or into His child, since the will of man is large enough while God's might is sufficient, and his aim is lofty, as it has been since the days of Adam and Cain. Yeshua wants me to believe this but I am only able to think and hope it. Surely thinking, hoping and loving are more sensible than believing?"

Menachem saw Miriam and some of her friends entering the square. How youthful she remained. As Miriam entered, people stood up. He left his place and followed her whom these people called "Mariam" in their Galilean dialect. The most Greek of them called her "Maria." She entered the long hall where the bride and bridegroom were lying on sofas while family members walked up and down, clustering about. Servants struggled to move through the groups of talking guests in order to fill their cups. Yeshua and his friends occupied the opposite sides of a long low table. His closest companion, the passionate and serious Yochanan, sat next to him; they formed a company within a company. But Jesus was not there for the companionship. Neither were his followers and students assembled for conversation but to be with him in order to see what he would reveal to them next. They told him about what the people were talking about and what was going on.

The woman of the house and mother of the bride who belonged to a much greater and wealthier family than poor Miriam of Joseph the carpenter, came up to her and bowed.

"What an honor, what an honor to see you here, mother of such a special son!" she welcomed her while bowing once more. Then a maidservant touched the arm of the baalath habayith,[2] telling her with a worried look:

"Madam, more and more guests are arriving but there are only two jars of wine left. What are we to do, what are we to do?" Miriam overheard the conversation.

"Let me ask my son. He knows so many people, he may be able to help." Miriam was pleased to get involved in this domestic affair and for the opportunity to offer assistance. She headed towards where Yeshua was sitting as the guests made way for her by pressing themselves against the wall. She thanked them with a friendly smile, not failing to notice their respect and thinking for a moment that she felt as comfortable with it as crossing the road in front of her humble house in Nazareth.

Reaching Yeshua, she laid her hand on his arm. He gave her a strange look, saying: "What have I to do with you, woman?" Then he closed his eyes, his head sank and he didn't immediately make the connection between the two different lives he was living. It wasn't always possible to step from the one into the other without a dizzy spell. Miriam gave her child a worried glance. She turned away, disguised her hurt and looked with reassuring confidence at the approaching master of ceremonies. "Do exactly as my son says, everything will be alright."

She left the hall, crossing the yard to a deserted space behind the house where two camels were standing.

"Miriam, Miriam!" She felt a hand in hers. It was Menachem behind her.

Miriam had been suppressing her feelings with great difficulty. Now she burst into tears.

"I know what you want to say: it is written: honor your father and your mother. Yeshua honors me but he could not help it. So perhaps he was in the one world and I was in the other world, Menachem?"

"You're right, Miriam. He had no choice. He's a good son as you know."

"He's so great yet so far away. Some people claim he's the Messiah. That is too great, Menachem. They say, 'Blessed be the womb that bore him.' Perhaps that is so. If that is the case, his mother must also make a great sacrifice. Sometimes I thank God for Yeshua's greatness, other times I say to myself: A good man, a good son, a good Jew would have been enough. I

---

2. Mistress of the household.

know very well, Menachem, that a Messiah cannot stay with his mother but a mother still remains a mother."

Then Miriam was silent for a while, before exclaiming as if the words were being wrenched from her: "Menachem, does Yeshua get angry because I remind him of the woman's body in which he lived? Does he not want to be reminded of the flesh? Woe is me, then I'd rather die so there's nothing to remind him of his human ancestry."

"Be comforted, Miriam, he does not want that. He has so much to do and is under such pressure that he cannot always be with you on account of the work."

Miriam grabbed his hand:

"Menachem, I wish you were my son too."

"It cannot be, Miriam. It's either Yeshua or Menachem," he said with humility. "I care for you very much and I admire your love for your son."

Miriam pressed Menachem's hand and returned to the feast. He thought, "Honor your father and your mother," says God. Can Yeshua do that, is he allowed to? He intends well, he chose God as his father. Yeshua is good to people but not to his own people. "What have I to do with you, woman?" He will have to leave Miriam in order to fulfill his task. But even Yeshua could not solve the contradiction between the son who stays with the family and takes care of his elderly parents as opposed to the one who leaves in order to pursue his destiny. Many tears are in store for Miriam.

"Menachem, Menachem, come and see!" yelled a gang of young Galileans who had seen him leaving. "Yeshua has performed a great miracle, he has changed water into wine so now there's enough for everybody." They were following him and stopped in front of him, surprised that Menachem was unmoved by the miracle. "Nay, Yeshua's intention is greater than what you saw," he told them. "He sees the emptiness, the need and the lack in peoples" lives and he wishes to fill them. Now he does it in the flesh but as he has told you, his concern is with the spirit."

"You don't believe that Yeshua is Messiah? Yet you are his friend!" the youngsters exclaimed in astonishment. "You envy him, Menachem! We didn't expect that of you," said one of them. Menachem raised and lowered his hand to calm them down.

"Did I say I don't believe that Yeshua is a Messiah? You are greedy guys, wanting everything at once. Would I be envious of Yeshua the—but you won't understand."

"What: the—?"

"Who wishes to do so much for humanity that he rises above the thought that not much can be done for the spawn of Cain, so high that he is prepared to fall down into death."

Menachem's glance into the future made him shudder.

3

HE WOULD NOT LET go. Like a leopard Menachem followed the track of Yeshua and his friends, sneaking around their camp at night until he found a hidden ditch where he slept and awoke before them.

For the moment they were moving south towards Judea and Jerusalem which still stood firmly on its hills despite the fact that little flames were licking at its walls on all sides. Menachem rejoiced in the sight of the city that he loved. Which mother bore so much, with so much pain!

Jerusalem was the epicenter of God's word. For centuries Jerusalem had been drawing God to her in desperate exaltation. That's why Yeshua had to take this route. Yeshua the Galilean approached her like a soldier whilst Menachem who was her child, accepted her ecstatic joys and her wild flaws. Her complexity was his simplicity.

Thus they went up to the Temple which appeared to be elevated by the city's strange glow. The Temple seemed to ascend up to heaven like a column of incense and simultaneously the Temple reeked. The Temple was purified by God's presence and the Temple smelled of idolatry. Where people wanted to transcend the human, their intentions split in two. Like a rocket, one part soared up to the sacred whilst the other tumbled down to the mundane. The Temple was great through its own extremes and through humanity's extreme yearning for God. It was the most imposing building on earth.

People ascended the stairs to the Temple like bees crawling up a honeycomb. They swarmed around it. They hallowed it with their loftiest emotions but they also wished to share their everyday feelings. God inspired awe but they had become familiar with him and desired that He also got to know and accept their flaws. On the side of the Golden Gate the sounds of animals filled the air, a moving blanket of lowing and bleating over the pilgrims. Their droppings formed islands on the ground surrounded by streams of yellow-green urine. It was a never-ending symphony of splashing, crying and bellowing whilst in front of the temple portico where the sacrificial animals were herded together, the donkeys brayed and the camels bleated and grunted.

Yeshua and his companions calmly passed this tumult that did not seem to bother him, the man from Galilee. The simplicity of life ought not to be disturbed overmuch by a drastic separation of the pure from the impure. That type of chasm which played such an important part in the view of the Pharisees was exactly what irritated him. Perhaps it reminded him of the separation of people into different classes which was a thorn in his side. It never occurred to him that the animal compound next to the House of God might be inappropriate. The moment he entered the vestibule he heard the shouting of the people. That pained him. Long rows of stalls were manned by serious merchants whose wild fingers stroked their musical beards. They were exchanging drachmas and talents that visitors to the Temple needed as gifts and offerings. Some merchants sold doves, so that the poor might also have something to offer to God. Although many in the temple precinct did not believe any more that God wanted doves, they could not say that since they knew the masses of people had a need to offer something. The poor man needed the means to establish a bond with God.

"Who needs my doves? The fragrance of their fat is more appealing than that of sheep!"

"Egyptian dinars are exchanged here!"

"I'm not giving you one more drachma."

"Their raised voices competed with one another in the house of God, quite naturally as they had been doing this daily for years. They were as familiar with this house as a gravedigger with corpses."

Yeshua, however, came from the wide land of Galilee and for him the Temple was a dream. Mankind's conscience was unclean. Could people not keep clean that one place that was dedicated to God? He loved the Temple and he loved Jerusalem. In his youth he saw the Temple from afar, rising over Mount Moriah. When he heard the hustle and bustle of trade instead of respectful whispers, fury took hold of him. Instead of the name Michael he heard "three shekels!" and instead of Gabriel he heard "fattened for two months," and instead of Seraphim and Mal'achim,[1] "six drachmas are enough!" The people haggled and argued away the sanctity of the place.

---

1. Angels.

Grabbing a stick, Yeshua yelled: "Get out, thieves, liars, robbers, you're defiling my Father's house!"

He overturned a stall; coins bearing Caesar's profile rolled across the floor. A dove cage was overturned, allowing the birds to flutter up to the ceiling. Inspired by his example, Jesus's companions got in on the act and soon row upon row of stalls had been overturned. Old merchants threw their arms in the air in despair at the fate of their wares. Their sons wanted to attack the Galileans.

"You're accusing us of being thieves! You are the destroyers and the robbers! You're taking away the livelihood of poor, hardworking people! Get out of here, Galileans!" There was great consternation on both sides.

Levites amongst the people alerted the police. Roman soldiers poured into the area to restore order.

How eagerly they did that and with how much contempt! They were the third party who did not understand the others, and then contempt came so easily, satisfying the soul with thickened oil.

Grabbing Jesus and his friends by the shoulders, the Roman soldiers dragged them down the temple terraces. When they reached the wide square below, the multitudes roared their approval. Jesus had punished those who cheated them out of their hard-earned money but the Romans were also evicting those traders from the temple precinct who had resisted the onslaught. These waved their fists at the Galileans, cursing them. The crowd surged closer around Jesus while chanting: "Hail the Prophet from Galilee! Keep helping us, Master!"

Some religious young men protested: "They praise them, even though they've desecrated the Temple with their violence and threats?"

Jesus came to, opening his eyes widely so that the Temple was swallowed by them. Then he exclaimed: "In truth, what is a Temple? A building of stone and iron. I tell you . . ." and he felt himself drifting upwards, higher and higher above the multitude where his face was refreshed by the height and the space . . . "I tell you, I will destroy and rebuild the Temple in three days!"

"He blasphemes!" cried the young Talmud students that loved the Temple and thought of its building stones as the flesh of God. The other people kept quiet, shocked by Jesus's statement. They applauded him when he chased merchants and embarrassed highly educated Pharisees but when he spoke of lofty metaphysical things, they became uneasy since they didn't understand what he meant or intended. People longed for a Messiah but what would the Messiah really do, what would he be like? They played with fire and this Jesus was now saying things that made the ordinary people back away as from the four letters of God's holy name.

Menachem had observed the tumult in the Temple. Mulling it over, he headed towards his mother's house. Rachel embraced him. She felt like a plant whose flower had returned to its leaves. A friend of his mother's was there, Sirach ben Yosef from Jericho, a moderate Pharisee from the school of Hillel.

"Great things are happening," Menachem said. "Is there something we need to discuss?" He was silent for a while then resumed: "History is made up of streams. But do the streams ever join together?"

"How do we know?" replied Sirach. "Events take place here and there and far from one another. But God, who arranged things, holds the cards. At the right moment he grabs them and presses them together into a single ball. Just like he hurls the sun through space, he hurls the ball of events into time until it falls apart again."

"That's possible," said Menachem.

Sirach continued: "It won't take so long anymore. The time of consolidation and casting away is approaching."

"Poor Israel," said Rachel.

"There are too many Jews that cannot wait any longer," Sirach remarked.

"That will always be so and they will always be necessary," observed Menachem.

"Ben Nesher could not wait. His time had come so he acted. Yeshua of Nazareth cannot wait. Today he has done great things."

"I already know," replied Sirach.

"All of these are coming out of Israel and they have nothing to do with one another."

"There are those who can indeed wait," resumed Sirach.

"I know—you, the Pharisees."

"We have the Law and the Law is eternal."

"What is the Law without life, Sirach ben Yosef?"

"The Law existed before the earth was created, Menachem."

"That's what the sages say but the Law was made for life, like the cradle for the child."

"Your son has lapsed from your father's Law, Rachel," Sirach said half in jest, half sadly.

"My child is no apostate. I raised him in my father's faith, in which he continues."

"I hear you are a friend of the prophet from Nazareth," said Sirach.

"I am his friend but he does not know it and does not want my friendship."

"Is Yeshua here?" asked Rachel. "I would love to see him again. I have such fond memories of him. Nothing bad can come from him. God's grace dwelt in his eyes and hands."

"I hear much good about him and much bad too," said Sirach ben Yosef. "In whose name does he really speak? Who was his teacher?"

"I don't know," replied Menachem. "But he knows the Law. I believe he has immersed himself in it and that his father has taught him the essence of it because he calls our Father his father."

"In whose name does he speak?" Sirach asked again.

"In his own name. That's why I believe in him although he does not find my faith good enough and despises it. Truly, the time has come. For ages people have been too inhibited in Israel. No one dared to speak in his own name. And it has gone so far that nobody has anything new to say anymore. Forgive me, Sirach, forgive me, mother. You are thinking of Hillel of blessed memory. Hillel was gentle and kind hearted. But the prophets spoke differently. Forgive me, Sirach. You have built too much on the Law. Yochanan the Baptist, from Beth Abara . . ."

"Herod Antipas has had him arrested."

"I know, Yochanan the Baptist and Yeshua of Nazareth have broken down the gate. They are doing the work of the time. Israel is ready to give birth. Do you not sense it? Perhaps Yeshua is indeed the Messiah as his followers believe."

"Beware of your words, Menachem."

"But why do you not come with?" said Menachem absent mindedly.

"What do you mean?"

"There are Pharisees that take up the sword against Rome—may their arms be blessed! Why are there no men of Yeshua's to break open the gates to freedom for Israel?"

"You say that we are blocked, that we throttle ourselves with the Law and the Law with commentary. I understand that. The word must build up first, tie in with another word, to make sense. Yet we have sinned so much,

Menachem, we have served idols, sinned with foreign women, plundered the poor, attached ourselves to Astarte, we have sinned so much. In that time the Prophets indeed spoke in their own names, inspired by God. Did the children of Israel improve through that? Then Ezra and Nehemiah arrived. They imprinted the Law in every fiber of our being. The Jews know now that they have to keep it, since sin still lies on the threshold of the mouth and the hands. Venus and Aphrodite and Bacchus and Pan have open temples. Rome beckons. Ten tribes have been lost. We have only two left: Judah and Benjamin. Would it not be better to hide in a cave where the air is oppressive but where we will save our lives than to stand in front of it and let ourselves be slaughtered? The time has not yet arrived, Menachem. *It is not yet possible.*"

"That is most unfortunate, Sirach. The time has arrived but the moment does not suit us. Alas, I see clearly now. The fruit of time hangs before us but we are not allowed to take it. Because if we dare go outside, the enemy will kill us. My God, my God, why has it not happened earlier and why could it not happen later?"

"Le Adonai Eloheinu haNestareth—the secrets belong to God," said Sirach, and continued: "If you are a friend of Yeshua, warn him. He has alienated many. They will unite against him. The Sadducees are afraid that Yeshua's activities have angered the Roman Governor while our people do not want the Law to be questioned anymore. Yeshua is looking for controversy."

"He seeks controversy," granted Menachem, "because he is controversial."

"I weep for Miriam that her son is in danger," said Rachel. "He is after all, one of the greatest of our time. Will he be able to help Israel?"

"No," Menachem replied.

"Then why does he endanger his life?"

"For the people," replied Menachem. Then, covering his eyes with his hands, "I see it now in all its clarity. Yeshua wishes to become the mediator; instead of Israel the people of God, Yeshua of Nazareth, the son of God."

"Yet he has friends who wish to advise and help him, even amongst us," Sirach said.

"Are you prepared to mention names?"

"I am amongst friends. Nicodemus, a member of the Sanhedrin and Joseph of Arimathea."

"It is good to know that," Menachem observed. "My task is impossible; I want to save Yeshua for Israel."

"If you are Yeshua's friend, accompany me tonight," Sirach asked. "I know where to find him, amongst friends of both his and ours. We could warn him to be more careful and not make such provocative statements."

"I know. He claimed that he could destroy the Temple and build it up again in three days."

"Was that not taking things too far?" asked Sirach. "Those who love God's temple do not play with it."

"Who had it rebuilt?" Menachem asked drily, answering his own question: "Herod, the bloodhound."

It was night. Sirach and Menachem draped themselves in cloaks. Rachel put on a black garment. They proceeded past the Roman bathhouse in a northerly direction along a deserted road. Before they reached the hill of the seers they turned west, all alone on this solitary road. The only person they encountered was a camel driver and his two animals.

Then they reached a garden surrounded by a stone wall in which Sirach found an opening. Beyond an olive grove stood a house belonging to what the Romans called a patrician. Flowers adorned the low balustrades. The house appeared to be more suited to joy than to gravitas, built for love rather than history. Passing through a gateway, they crossed a square laid out with Italian marble and reached an oval room.

"These are friends," said Sirach before those present could ask. In the room stood Nicodemus, the member of the Sanhedrin, his son-in-law Antonius ben Philippos HaGe'er, Joseph of Arimathea and two other high officials from Jerusalem.

"Where is Yeshua?" whispered Rachel. Then she saw him, all in white, standing against a red curtain that divided this oval room either from outside or from another room. Next to him was his young friend Yochanan with the black curls, the one Menachem had heard being called the apostle John.

A long silence followed their arrival although Menachem sensed that much had been said before they entered.

Rachel approached Yeshua.

"Yeshua!"

"Who are you?"

"But Yeshua, don't you recognize the mother of Menachem? I am Rachel."

"I only know those who come to take from me. *Those who think that they can give me something, I do not know.*"

"Yeshua, between you and me there's no question of give and take," whispered Rachel.

"The woman is arrogant," Yeshua said to Yochanan.

Shocked, Rachel moved back towards her son, who told her: "He is taking up his destiny, do not think that he is rude."

"I told my friend from Nazareth that he must leave Jerusalem, that danger awaits him here," said Nicodemus. "However, he pointed out to me that he was sent to do his Father's will." He had barely said that when a white light filled the room. Menachem, besides himself, exclaimed: "Yeshua, Yeshua, save yourself, for the sake of Israel!"

"Who are you?" asked Jesus. Menachem went and stood right in front of him, saying:

"Why are you denying me?"

"Must I say it again? Because you do not believe in me!"

Suddenly Menachem looked like Yeshua and said in a voice that resembled his:

"Yeshua, Yeshua, Do you have need of so much faith? Surely you do not doubt yourself? Why do you need more faith than God?"

"Not me—you need faith," Jesus replied, and Menachem answered: "My faith is sufficient. No container can hold more than its capacity."

Then the strange light, the white light, disappeared from the room and again it was night. Servants brought two candelabras with candles.

Menachem didn't know whether the others had seen the light and heard his own words and those of Yeshua but he noticed that they had changed places. Nicodemus and Joseph of Arimathea now stood next to Jesus whilst Sirach stood by the door.

The weeping Rachel held on to the red curtain with both hands in order to stay upright.

In the middle of the room stood Menachem. His love was on both sides. He realized that much love also builds a wall around a person that makes one feel alone and isolated.

4

FROM THEN ON MENACHEM knew that he had to prevent something on behalf of Yeshua and on behalf of Israel. However, the thought of it filled him with despair, as if it were a hopeless mission. They were one in order to be separated and separated in order to remain one.

Menachem still followed Yeshua and his companions. They saw him walking on the mountain paths with his figure supple like lichen. The disciples pretended not to notice since they were of the opinion that their Master did not approve of him. At present they were passing through Samaria which a Jew tried to avoid as it was thought to be a dangerous and unholy region. The Samaritans accepted the Faith but did not grant Israel any right to it. Samaria was an illegitimate son that despised the true son and wished to replace him. They harassed Jewish travelers, mocked the pilgrims, and threw stones at the women. Yeshua was unconcerned about the dangers. He didn't move faster neither did he linger, he had his established way of walking and living that he did not change for storm or foe.

At the well of Jacob near Sichar the company halted and Menachem concealed himself in a hollow. The Galileans went to the city to get food. The air hung hot over the meandering mountains stretched out like a crocodile. A Samaritan woman approached along one of the mountain trails on her way to the well. She kneeled, lowered her water jars and started to fill them. She was beautiful with passionate but unhappy eyes. She resented living through and for men, viewing it as a daily burden. Menachem crept closer, reaching the ridge behind the well where he lay like a lizard.—"Please give me some water," he heard Yeshua say. She glanced at him with annoyance. "Why should I?" she replied, "I don't know you. Go and ask for water in Jerusalem!"

"You do not know me," said Jesus. "If you knew me, you would ask me for water. Those who drink the water I give, never thirst again." His hands drew a bow-shape in the air. "Everybody has something to do with me—and all people are connected. The woman is Samaritan and I am a Jew. Where is the division? The woman is unclean and my mother is clean, where is the divide?" The woman noticed that Jesus was a handsome man in the prime of his years. He had beautiful eyes. She wanted to stare him down but could not. "Retreat," she told herself, something she was not used to do. Then she lowered her eyes and poured some water for Jesus. After having drunk, he said: "Go fetch your husband so he may get some water too."

"I don't have a husband," she answered. "You've had five and the one you're living with now is not your husband," Jesus said drily without a hint of condemnation. "Go then and do not tell anyone whom you have met." "I know Mosheach must come," she said, "to teach us many things. Are you him?"

But Yeshua wasn't listening anymore and called on his returning disciples that they had to be moving on.

When they had gone some distance, Menachem got up and stared after the Samaritan woman—much of the defiance had gone out of her walk. Yeshua had taken a huge step forward when he spoke to this woman. Yeshua is Israel that has gone to the nations! It is high time for this to happen since the nations cannot wait any longer. But it would have been better had Yeshua not spoken to the woman about the spirit of God. She's an enemy of Israel and the nations crave Israel's well. They are thirsty, they want to drink up the source and kill Israel. Yeshua had taken the first step of a process that cannot be stopped but for Israel it is too early. Woe to the woman that gives premature birth and the child that is born too soon! But Yeshua said: "The manger is ready and the Father calls for his child." My God, why did you not arrange the same time for Israel and the nations and why do you cast your child Yeshua between two opposite streams of your time?

Back in Galilee, Yeshua and his disciples immediately went to the synagogue of Kefar Nachum, which was called Capernaum by the Romans. He was well known in this town on the shore of Lake Genesareth.[2]

Yeshua had barely entered the synagogue which looked like a white box from the outside, when there was a stirring in the congregation to reach his presence. While the rabbi was reading from the Prophets, the people stopped listening. Jesus and his disciples were of greater interest.

2. Lake Kinnereth.

To his dismay, Menachem observed a man in a corner of the synagogue that he had noticed earlier. He remembered the face from the occasion in the temple when Jesus confronted the merchants. Then the man also stood leaning against a pillar and sneering. Now he was snickering again because no one was listening to the rabbi. The man was lean and tall with hollow cheeks, prominent chin, connected eyebrows, a thin nose and thick lips. He looked mean.

Menachem reflected on what a strange web of disdain and respect existed among the people. He had recognized the rabbi—Abba Alexander, the father of his friend Yocheved. Now this Pharisee was a pious and respectable man, whilst the fellow who was snickering because Jesus took the attention away from Abba Alexander, had a malicious air about him. Yet at times he gave Yeshua glances of approval and admiration. And Menachem realized that this man justified his contempt for Abba Alexander through his admiration for Jesus. The congregation surged forward like a wave. When Jesus and his company had entered, a spark of hope arose in old Jonah ben Tarfon whose hand was shriveled and lame. He would have loved to run to the front, to the strange young prophet, but he dared not. So he made it clear to those around him that he was reluctant but desired to have his hand healed and they responded by taking him towards Jesus.

"What's wrong?" Jesus asked when he saw him approaching hesitantly with the others pushing him forward.

"Master, his hand is lame. For twenty years his hand has been dry like a camel's jawbone in the desert!"

"Lift your hand! You are healed."

Hallelujah, it was healed!

Around him the people started talking and expressing their admiration. And soon they started arguing. Some claimed that they had always said that this son of Joseph the carpenter of Nazareth was a prophet and that the others had eyes but did not see. The man is no ordinary prophet, the man is the Messiah! Blessed are we, to see him with our own eyes!

The mean fellow had also joined Jesus's admirers but on the spot where Abba Alexander had been reading from the Prophets, a group of Pharisees was making their disapproval clear.

Whether it was them that persuaded Abba Alexander to protest, Menachem didn't know. The strict Pharisee with his dark eyes and square beard confronted Yeshua: "Why did you interrupt the reading of the word of God?" Returning his gaze without flinching, Jesus replied: "The word of

God is still being revealed. Is there no Oral Law?" Abba did not reply as he agreed that God's word also spoke through the commentaries. He had meant something else by his admonition. The prophet from Nazareth was wiser than him.

"Why do you defile the Sabbath?"

"I healed the man's hand."

"Could it not wait until tomorrow?"

"Nay!"

"It is written: but the seventh day you will remember to hallow!" Abba told Jesus.

Then the mocking laughter of the strange, tall man was heard. "Tell me why the Sabbath was created? Was the day created for mankind or was mankind made for the day?" Jesus asked Abba Alexander.

"The Sabbath is the will of God! People exist in order to do God's will. But it is useless arguing with you; you do not want to understand us."

Deeply offended, Abba Alexander turned away. Yeshua and the son of the Herodian Marcus Mercator, who stood by as a type of witness, were younger than the rabbi. It appeared as though respect for age had vanished from Israel.

Outside the town, Yeshua and his disciples were walking in the fields of ripened corn. The Sabbath hung like a canopy over the time-span that it covered. High above the field, rosy flamingoes flew towards Lake Kinnereth. Here and there little bluebirds fed on the ripe ears of corn. Jesus and his disciples walked in the midst of the field. Far behind, the unbidden follower Menachem got a fright. Who was walking next to Yeshua? The man that he first noticed when Jesus reprimanded the temple merchants and again this morning in the synagogue. "This is the real desecration of the Sabbath," thought Menachem. "The man next to Yeshua, he is sacrilege!"

Then the Sabbath was further dishonored. Jesus's followers must have been hungry, as they started plucking ears of corn to chew the seed. Adjacent to the field ran a road where those who had attended the synagogue service that morning took an afternoon stroll. They took umbrage when they saw what the followers of Jesus were doing, thereby disturbing their own rest and that of the plants. Once again the hoary, weighty arguments between Jesus and the Pharisees came up. These quarrels were worse than plucking ears of corn.

Menachem complained to himself: "Life afflicts itself. Lightning shatters the sky, storms disturb the tranquil reflection of the lake. Quarrels between the children of Israel during the summer of the prophet from Nazareth!" And Menachem started reflecting on all the evil in the world. Paradise has been ruined. In order to make human life possible, it was necessary to mix black and white and add blood to the blue of heaven. Since the days of Adam and Cain people had need of unrest. But there was too much dark. Menachem started lamenting the irony in the ancient sing-song style:

The Song of Menachem

> Oh Lord, evil had to enter the world so that we would not burst from one-sided joy. If you, however, had sent us only death, it would have been enough!
>
> And if you had sent us only anxiety over the well-being of those we love, it would have been enough!
>
> And that we had to experience Rome's victory over Israel, that would have been enough!
>
> And that you created the people of Israel with sin in our hearts while expecting us to be a nation of priests, truly that would have been enough!
>
> And that you placed the fear in our people that they would succumb to sins that they cannot avoid, truly that would have been enough!
>
> And that you made mothers and fathers plead anxiously for their children to follow the good road in order to live!
>
> That you let us shake and tremble with uncertainty whether our nation Israel would choose the good way and live or the evil way and perish. Truly, these fears would have been enough!
>
> Enough of the shadow was given us so that your sun would not shine too brightly!
>
> And that you had Yeshua born at a time when your nation Israel was forced to close themselves up even more in order not to fall apart, instead of opening their hearts to him. Surely that would have been enough for us!
>
> And that you brought Yeshua in conflict with the Pharisees and caused conflict between Yeshua's love for you and the Pharisees' love for you so the one did not respect the other's love, truly that would have sufficed for us!
>
> And that after centuries you sent a Messiah who says it is not enough to believe in you and that he is part of you, after we had been forged in fire and flame to hallow your name only, truly, that snare would have been enough for us!

And that you demand faith from mankind while not giving faith, surely, that would have sufficed as shade so that the sun does not shine too brightly.

And that you defiled your son Yeshua by placing in his company a thug that would at the same time destroy Israel and Yeshua, and that you combined black and white in those that you sent, truly after such a long yearning for a Messiah, that would have been enough!

Since Adam and Eve left paradise Satan had to be with us as we do not breathe freely when there's no poison in the air. But has the poison not become too much on this Sabbath while we walk across this field under the circling eagles? Is this an hour of redemption?

Yeshua was laying his hand on the shoulder of the sneering man when the Sabbath guards were approaching under Abba Alexander. "Why do your pupils defile the holy Sabbath?" asked Abba. "They were hungry," Jesus replied, "and what did David do when he was hungry? Did he not eat of the showbread meant for the priests? He also gave his men some of it. Was that permitted by the Law?" Then Jesus gave Abba Alexander a look of disdainful compassion, saying:

"But I am more than the Temple and master over the Law."

Abba Alexander shook his head. "Why then do you give the people a bad example, encouraging them to break the Law? Why is the first thing you teach the people is to break the Law of Him who sent you? And if you are not the Messiah then what benefit do you see in the fact that our people discard the lessons that our ancestors learnt through so many trials? That you try to humiliate us will be forgiven but your contempt for God's Law is on your head."

Jesus answered: "That you sin against me, Pharisee, that is forgiven, but that you sin against the Holy Spirit, that is on your conscience."

Abba Alexander shrugged his shoulders as he did not understand this conversation anymore and Jesus had turned away from him, followed by his disciples.

Menachem continued to follow the Master and his disciples, mumbling his sad refrain that reflected what he had seen: "*That which one loves is the prey of his brother.*"

Then he noticed that someone was walking alongside him. Giving him a sidelong glance, Menachem recognized the man who had snickered in the temple when Yeshua confronted the merchants and the same one who had beamed with happiness when people stopped paying attention to Abba Alexander in the synagogue.

Apparently the man had intentionally stayed behind in order to talk to Menachem. "I have been aware of you for a long time," said the strange, mocking companion of Yeshua. "You are always following our Master. Who are you?"

"What is your name?" Menachem asked in return.

"My name? Everyone knows that: Judas, the man from Karioth."

"What, your name is Judas?"

"Aye, why so surprised?"

"I am, indeed."

"Why?"

"Yehudah is a good name," said Menachem. "That was the name of the mighty Maccabee. Are you as brave as the mighty Maccabee?"

"I am more of a follower." He snickered again.

"Were you born under the sign of the Lion?" asked Menachem.

"Nay!" Judas pulled a pious face but behind the sanctimony there seemed to be a mix of sadness and faith.

"I was born under the sign of the Lamb."

"Yehudah is not the right name for you, Judas. Your father did not know what he was doing when he named you—or he knew all too well."

"Do you have a more suitable name for me?"

"Aye, Korach."

"Korach, Korach—that was the man who plagued Moses." Judas sneered.

"I have yet another name for you, a name that no one in Israel has ever had, Judas. A name that also suits you well."

"Tell me."

"Ohyev."

"Ohyev, the enemy? A strange name, that is true. How do you know that I am an enemy?"

"I'm guessing, Judas. I know whose enemy you are."

"The Pharisees."

"That's true. But you are the enemy of others too. You are the enemy of . . ."

The eyes of Judas took on an evil aspect and his lower jaw sagged while his thick tongue protruded from his mouth.

"Don't you dare say it, don't you dare, accursed son of a bitch!"

"You are the enemy of every plant that bears flowers, if I may put it like that, Judas Iscariot. Have I guessed correctly?"

Judas closed his mouth and resumed: "I saw you in the Temple. What a lovely sight it was when the coins rolled in all directions. I know very well how greedy they are about every coin—no one knows better than I. One of them stood crying—old Abraham ben Aryeh HaBavli—since he owns nothing else besides the doves he was selling. Is our Master not grand, is he not glorious? You must have noticed this morning how he shut up the old Pharisee Abba Alexander? I don't like the Pharisees, I hate them!"

"Why, Judas?"

"You know that as well as I, stranger. They think too highly of themselves. They think they are assisting God. Jesus hates that too; he dislikes people that think so much of themselves. Jesus and I hate the same people. I love him more than my life because he's better than those who are so smug. Do you know what the Master will do with the Pharisees? He will cast them into the pit."

"Judas, Judas," Menachem replied. "Pay attention to my words. You are a Nazarene with the Pharisees and a Pharisee with the Nazarenes. What will you do when it goes well with Jesus? I call you the enemy."

"Man oh man," Judas taunted Menachem.

"How yellow you are; you're as yellow as sulfur."

"What has skin color to do with it Judas? Did the Shulamite woman not exclaim: 'I am dark but beautiful?'"

"Yes, yes, Jerusalemite. You know scripture but you're as yellow as sulfur, from envy."

Again Judas gave a sneering laugh. When the sound abated, his mouth was still opening and closing. He had already lost many teeth and in their place the flesh was dark like that of a jackal. Age was already showing in his still young face.

"I'm not envious, Judas Iscariot. Who would I envy? No one in Israel could be envied at this time and I do not want to be a idolator."

"You're envious of me."

"Envious of you? I don't think anyone who has heard or seen you could be envious of you."

"You're envious of my place in the Master's circle. He doesn't want you. I'll ask him why you're not allowed and will return to tell you."

Again he cackled before setting off on a trot to catch up with Jesus and the disciples and to show Menachem that he belonged with the Master.

Menachem was troubled by the man's display of loyalty to Jesus. "I do not have envy but why is Yeshua so affectionate to the wicked fool? Does he want to show that he can make an instrument of anyone? One is a staff to him, one a hammer and another a dagger. See how his one hand rests on the shoulder of Judas and the other on that of Yochanan. I sense great evil arising for Israel from this unhealthy friendship between Yeshua and Judas Korach. I won't grant him the name of the Lion and the Maccabee. Satan inspired Judas's father to name him so. But that Yeshua, an expert reader of character, fails to perceive what is so obvious, astonishes me. What a web of evil is being spun around my people. I fear the threads will meet in a rope around the neck of Israel.

The world is made up of millions of threads and they readily entwine, usually to ill effect. Would it not be better if all these millions of threads formed a pattern that led to good? My friend Yeshua despairs so much over people for whom not much can be done, that he is determined to give them hope. So he wants to unite all the threads in himself to bring salvation. He has concluded correctly that I do not believe. I do not and will not believe because there's too much benevolence in Yeshua. Why is there no man who will stand up to sever the cord and destroy the snare that is forming to trap Yeshua and Israel? The Deity builds people into history, yet He does not build the whole of history on one son of man, Yeshua!"

At sunset Menachem noticed that Yeshua and his men started ascending a wide mountain that towered over the plain. He crept up behind them and was lucky enough to find a hiding place close to where they were sharing a meal near the summit. There was peace all around.

The disciples lay near their shepherd like contented sheep. They were chewing fish but Jesus was not eating. Looking at the little flock, he seemed to derive pleasure from their presence.

That is the Kingdom of God that he always speaks about, thought Menachem. It is in us and around us, but is it always like that? What surrounds us even more is the Roman Empire, the advancing waves of history and the evil of mankind. Yeshua said that the Kingdom of God is in us but I think it is an island and that there are many other islands in the ocean within us and around us.

When the disciples had eaten they remained lying there, eventually falling asleep under the stars. Menachem rested in his hiding place, close to them yet separated.

They awoke as they had fallen asleep, peacefully assembled around their master. The morning was bright and when the run had risen, friends and followers of Jesus came from all sides, from Judea and Galilee and from Tyre and Sidon, the cities on the coast. They ascended the broad slope of the mountain and settled down like the stones of a sanctuary. So many people had arrived that it appeared as if Jesus himself had reached his peak. As he stood staring straight ahead, he would occasionally stretch out his arms and open his hands as if his words were flowing through his body and dropping from his hands like raindrops from branches:

"Blessed are the poor in spirit for theirs is the kingdom of heaven."

Menachem thought: "In truth, they are blessed. But those who seek, bear and suffer are worthy to become blessed."

"Blessed are those who mourn," said Jesus, "for they will be comforted. Blessed are the gentle, for they shall inherit the earth."

"Amen, amen," replied Menachem and felt tears in his eyes, since he yearned for gentleness amongst his people.

"Do not think that I came to abolish the Law or the Prophets. I did not come to abolish but to fulfill. For truly I say to you, until heaven and earth pass away, not the smallest iota or tittle shall pass from the Law until all is accomplished. Whoever keeps and teaches them, he shall be called great in the Kingdom of Heaven."

"Yeshua, you confuse me! One cannot simultaneously live within and outside the Law!" thought Menachem.

"And when you pray, do not use meaningless repetition as the Gentiles do, for they suppose that they will be heard for their many words."

"Alas, we also assume that," thought Menachem, "and we act like the idolators and insult God in that way."

After that, Jesus told them a sound and simple prayer which Menachem memorized, holding Yeshua close to his heart.

"This prayer is acceptable to God, like a table laden for mankind!" he thought and his heart melted with tenderness.

"Look at the birds of the air, they do not sow nor reap nor gather into barns, and yet your heavenly Father feeds them." At that moment, black and white cranes were circling over the mount.

"And why are you worried about clothing? Observe the lilies of the field. They do not toil nor do they spin, yet I say to you that not even Solomon wore garments as splendid as that."

"How tender is his trust and how comforting to the individual," thought Menachem. But in the distance the trumpets of a Roman legion could be heard.

"God is good, even towards the ungrateful and the wicked," Jesus continued.

Menachem bowed down, thinking "Now mankind is taught aright. Now a new world is beginning. Yeshua, Yeshua, God speaks through you."

But then Jesus said: "Enter through the narrow gate because the large gate and the wide path lead to perdition and many are those who take it. The small gate and the narrow path lead to life and few are those who find it."

Menachem, who had stood up again, thought: "Yeshua, you confuse my soul. If you came to show the broad way then I understand your commission, but if you came to indicate the narrow way, why do you rail against the Pharisees?"

And Menachem told himself the following parable:

"There were two shepherds both of whom had good sheep. The one shepherd had to look after one thousand sheep and the other after fifty. The master said to the one with a thousand: 'Choose the wide road to come to me as on the narrow way your thousand will trample one another and fall into the abyss.' To the one with fifty he said: 'You choose the narrow way to come to me as your fifty sheep will get lost on the broad way and one would not be able to find them.' But the shepherd of the narrow way may not command the shepherd of the broad way: 'You do not know the will of my Master,' and the shepherd of the broad way may not accuse the one of the narrow way: 'You do not know the will of my Master.' Because both of them know it!"

"You have heard the teaching," assumed Jesus, "'you shall not commit adultery.' But I say to you that everyone who looks at a woman with desire has already committed adultery in his heart."

In the one-sided dialogue in his mind, Menachem replied: "Yeshua, why do you make the Guilt heavier, just like the Pharisees do to the Law?"

But Jesus continued, "You were taught to love your neighbor as yourself but I tell you: Love your enemy as yourself and do good to those that hate you. Bless them that curse you and pray for those that insult you."

Menachem replied: "Yeshua, why do you make the Obligation heavier just like the Pharisees do to the Law?"

He wondered about the quarrel between Jesus and the Pharisees. Why does he oppose them while associating with the tax collectors and the women of ill repute? Blessed be his open arms—"Those women and those tax collectors have nothing, Menachem—I fill their empty hearts."

"And the Pharisees, Yeshua? Why do you oppose them?"

"The Pharisees have too much. They must give me a place in their hearts but they refuse."

"Yeshua, Yeshua, you have uttered words of beauty but they will also attract their gatekeepers and their soldiers. And they will also have scribes guarding them. After the butterflies have visited the flower, the ants will come. When it has dried, they carry it off to the anthill. So spare the Pharisees for the sake of your Father and for their love of words. Do not complete what you have intended to do."

Suddenly someone grabbed Menachem by the ears. It was Judas, sneering through his missing teeth:

"I saw you beggar! I noticed that you were following us and that you slept in the ditch last night. Guess what the Master said?" Judas let out a hideous cackle: "Judas is dearer to me than Menachem for Menachem loves me, but Judas believes in me."

"Correct," said Menachem as he rose threateningly. "If he were God he would love me in response to my love. But the Son of Man thirsts for faith."

"Quiet, denier," Judas hissed, "or I'll kill you."

"Admit it, Judas Korach, you enjoy it when someone is humiliated!"

"Accursed son of a bitch! No no no! I believe in my Master. He is God's only son. Shut up or I'll throttle you! I care for him, I believe in him, he is all that I have, he is my wealth and my crown and my citizenship and all that I possess."

"He already means far too much to you, Judas. He owns too much in the world."

"Dirty beggar, spy, I'll strangle you!"

"Yes, do that," Menachem replied, "strangle me! Perhaps that will open Yeshua's eyes so that I may save him and Israel."

"No you deceiver, you want to hand me over to the Romans, I know. I'm going back to my Master and you, unbeliever, can die."

The multitude that had come to listen to Jesus was dispersing. On the Magdala road to Capernaum, Menachem took a side road towards the lake. In the distance the trumpets of a Roman cohort could be heard while thousands of birds were singing along the shores. He saw some fisherman boarding a boat and as he approached, he recognized the disciples—Peter, Yochanan and Nathaniel. Jesus was not amongst them. At his feet he saw a tiny raft between the reeds. He hopped on, loosened the rope and rowed after the large boat. All was tranquil until a black cloud suddenly appeared, covering the lake, followed by flashes of lightning and rolling thunder. In a short while the surface became turbulent. Huge waves surged and crashed against one another. Menachem kept rowing through the crests and the troughs. He was not worried even though the waves slapped his body and battered his little raft.

The night sky covered Lake Kinnereth. The lovely shore was obscured but a ray of white light connected heaven and water like a cleft in the night, like a chasm in death, a long, thin and endless window. In that light Menachem saw the boat with the disciples. They were wailing and crying, "Help, help, we're lost! O God of Israel, help your children!" Menachem recognized the deep bass voice of Peter but couldn't distinguish any of the other voices in the tumult. Another huge wave threw the boat up in the air again. Menachem had never experienced such an awesome moment. Despite the danger, he stood up on his little raft; what did he have to fear? And suddenly he saw inside the ray of light . . . his friend Yeshua, stretching out his arms and exclaiming, "Is that your faith?"

Then the dark clouds rolled away and the heaven returned to a shiny blue, revealing the picturesque shore of Lake Kinnereth with its patchwork of vegetation and hamlets. Yeshua was sitting amongst his men and Menachem smiled. Where was the faith of the disciples when the lake was being battered by the storm?

Menachem had not feared: Yeshua has not completed his course, neither have I, so what was there to fear?

God does not build history on one person, He builds people into history but the people concerned do not come loose by accident, least of all the foundation stones.

One man stood up in the boat and started shouting. "Ha, you're over there beggar, I saw you! You've followed us again, haven't you? You were afraid." Then he started making dance moves in the boat. "You are not allowed here. There's space in the boat but you're not allowed. Wouldn't you have loved to join us, beggar?"

Menachem recognized Judas who was jumping for joy on the boat but he couldn't see Yeshua anymore. The two craft reached the shore. Menachem remained standing where he had tied his little raft. Simon Peter bore down on him followed by Bartholomew and Yochanan, Judas, Thomas and another also called Yehudah. Peter grabbed Menachem by the chest.

"Did you see Yeshua on the water?"

"Aye."

"Do you believe now?"

"Who tells you that I do not believe? I believe more and I believe less than you."

"Jerusalemite snake, you always speak in riddles."

"Tell me Simon Peter, what is sacred, belief or a specific type of belief?"

"Shut up snake! Once again, "did or did you not see Jesus walking on the water?"

"I have seen his spirit, replied Menachem."

"I asked if you saw Yeshua."

"His spirit, Simon Peter, yet that is not enough for you. The Master teaches that we must learn to discern the spirits but if I see spirit and you see matter, you curse me and call me an unbeliever."

"You denier, you who refuse to admit what your eyes have seen. I feel like throwing you in the water."

Peter shook him violently—Menachem did not resist but endured it with a smile as he loved Simon Peter too.

"There is something you cannot kill, Simon Peter."

"What is that?"

"The Holy Spirit which watches over Israel from the beginning to the end of days. It is one thing to kill the individual spirit and another thing to kill the divine spirit contained in a people."

Peter recoiled, replying, "Amen." He loosed his grip on Menachem.

"The Holy Spirit is everywhere," mumbled another apostle, "not only in Israel."

"That is true, Matthew Levi, that is true!" exclaimed Menachem, "although its outpouring is not the same. The one happens in one person, the other in an entire nation. As Yochanan the Baptist said, 'God can make children for Abraham from the stones.' I am sure of this: Spirit is not blood and blood is not spirit but where blood and spirit combine, then there is rejoicing among the Seraphim."

The apostles retreated. They did not know anymore whether this Menachem was holy or blasphemous. At times it seemed that the voice of Yeshua was speaking through him and at other times it seemed as if he were talking like the Pharisees.

Menachem knew that they did not understand him. Because he did not wish to appear secretive, he told them:

"I choose Israel. Do you understand that? Listen, the mother does not want to give birth as she fears the child would murder her. Yet the mother will give birth and stay alive and my friend Yeshua will lift you up and prosper you outside of Israel. That is the will of God, but it breaks my heart."

"May you die, you dog!"

Judas had worked up spittle in his mouth and when he had had enough, he spat in Menachem's face.

BOOK FOUR

Parallel Roads Go Out From Golgotha

1

PASSOVER WAS APPROACHING. MASSES of people were flocking to Jerusalem to celebrate the festival of freedom in the land that had no liberty. The festival did not reflect reality. Reality however, is subordinate to loss for it fails to move the spirit in the same way as that which has been lost. A celebration of freedom is never observed as intensely as a commemoration of the yearning for freedom. The indifferent were absent; those who flocked to Jerusalem were the committed, the angry, those who longed and pleaded, and above all the concerned and the anxious. Time uses souls like pots on a stove in which feelings are prepared. With these feelings they reproduce themselves again.

Many people, country folk and workers in particular, were hoping that Jesus of Nazareth would come to Jerusalem. Even amongst the aristocrats and the educated there were numerous individuals who longed for his presence as he comforted afflicted souls and supported those who were falling. Thus far he had not taken up arms like Samson or ended the rule of the Romans but he intended something significant and possessed an immeasurable ability to attract the interest of others. He was there, he walked, ate, slept, spoke. Israel was too alone. Someone had come who dared to speak by his own authority—Yeshua, haNavi[1] haMosheach, hosanna hosanna!

Yeshua taught them and got to know them. Many had called him Messiah. He knew the Law and the Prophets. Often he quoted from Isaiah:

"For he grew up before The Eternal as a sapling, as a shrub out of dry ground. He had neither comeliness nor splendor that we should look up to him, nor beauty that we should admire him. He was despised and rejected by men. He was a man of grief and acquainted with sorrow, like one from whom people turn their faces away. He was despised, and we did not reckon him highly. Yet he did bear our diseases and took our pains upon himself. We considered him stricken, smitten and afflicted by God. But it

1. The prophet.

was because of our transgressions that he was wounded, on account of our iniquities that he was crushed. The punishment that brings us peace was upon him, and healing flows from his wounds."

Jesus meditated upon the words of Isaiah and said: "It will indeed be like that, thus I am the Messiah." That was his earthly side, his responsibility towards people. Jesus also felt immeasurable tenderness towards the other side, to God. All of his protective power was spread over the people. All of his need to be comforted, his devotional love and his obedience—nothing in the world was great enough for this—went forth to Him whom he called His Father.

He reminded God of his love. His deeds reflected what was written. He did not come to do away with the Law and the Prophets. That's why he held fast to the prophecies of Scripture. So he had his apostles fetch a donkey for him, a humble, sad and long-suffering animal on which he rode, accompanied by his men, to Jerusalem.

A sea of people surrounded them. They were filled with joy for Yeshua had come. The garments, the coats, the tunics fluttered around him like large beating wings. There came the stretchers bearing cripples whose faces were contorted with unanswered supplication. Hand-in-hand like children, long queues of the blind stumbled on. Lepers came, with holes in their flat noses or resembling lions or monkeys after having lost their noses and lips. People made way for them so that they were able to get close to Yeshua. The insane, with ropes around their bodies, were led by fathers or brothers. But the disfigured and the disturbed represented only tiny strands of grey in hair that was still black because around the Master heaved masses of yearning people, shouting: "Hosanna, Rabbinu, Hosanna, Adoneinu!"[2]

From the back of the little donkey Jesus looked over the undulating waves of people and his heart was troubled. The people were suffering so much. God was silent. There were no kings. Instead time had forced the Herodians, the bitter pill of strangers, into their mouth. The throat of Israel, however, was too narrow to swallow this pill. Besides, King David and Judah the Maccabee lived in their memory. They longed for a friend of God, a mediator; their grief was too profound for them to express it themselves. The Faith was threatened by the Romans at the gate of the Temple. At night they went to bed afraid of the soldiers who might take them away. And within them dwelt the weariness of the long ages of struggle to keep God and not to lose Him again. Now they were too exhausted to bear their

2. "Our Lord."

treasure or the fear that the treasure would be stolen: "Hosanna, Rabbinu, hosanna Yeshua!"

"My God, my God, what can I do for them?" pleaded Yeshua. "I can bring them to you but no more. I will bring them. But they won't believe me if I don't put them first. They want what I cannot give and what I can give, they're not interested in. I want to give them everything, my life if it may be of benefit to them, my flesh and blood, every fiber of my flesh and every drop of my blood. Yes, let every strand of my flesh become a chain that binds thousands to you and let every drop of my blood become a sea in which they may wash off their sins. More I cannot give, my God. I admit that. With my life I can do less than with my death. So please take me to you, Father, as I am prepared to die for them."

Menachem was walking alone amongst the multitudes, lean, young and swarthy. He saw Jerusalem lying on her hills, both peaceful and threatening. Reaching for the sun in one place, rooted to the soil in another whilst further along the city was spread out comfortably wide. Jerusalem with the Temple, the priestly palaces, the palace of Herod and the palaces of the Maccabees with their gates and fountains. He saw all the multitudes who had already encamped in front of the city as well as the approaching groups and caravans.

Jesus looked around and his grief turned to hope. "My God, my God, there's still much to gain," he said as he turned his eyes to the west and the sea and to the north, to Mount Hermon. But Menachem who was bearing the sorrow of all the people who were coming up to celebrate Pesach, saw them and felt them like an approaching hurricane. Looking at the golden domes of Jerusalem. He sighed: "My God, my God, we fear that we stand on the edge of Gehennom[3] but we're still close to your heaven. Bless us, bless us, there's still so much to be lost."

The crowds also contained those who were called "troublemakers" by Rome, the proconsul and Herod the fox. And there were many soldiers about, disguised as Roman civilians, Arabs, Jews in Greek tunics or like Jews of the land. The simple people were rushing to the public baths. They felt the joy of Passover. For them and their Pharisee teachers the world was made up of two levels: that of daily life and that of the Torah. The lower level of daily life was somber and steadily losing its appeal, being the dimension of oppression and the lack of freedom. Above that was life in the Law, a garden of delight with fragrant flower-beds. The flower-beds

3. Hell.

around the garden path were the Sabbaths. The flower-beds in the middle were the festivals; the happiest one with the tallest flowers was Passover. The distance between the two dimensions was constantly increasing. The lower level was losing appeal to many of the pharisaic persuasion whilst the garden above was looking ever more appealing. Yet life was below and the Law above.

Menachem negotiated the crowds to get close to Jesus who was riding peacefully as his supporters opened the way before him.

"He could have himself crowned as King of the Jews," thought Menachem. "With his many friends he could attempt a revolution but then the Romans would come and punish Israel."

Near Menachem a man cried in agony and collapsed. Simultaneously two men in nomad's attire grabbed hold of a young man. The area became a swirling vortex as people crowded around to watch.

"He stabbed Antonius Scriptor to death."

"Who?"

"That one they're holding. Another one of the agitators of Yehuda the Galilean!"

"One less thug in Jerusalem isn't worth the life of a young man."

"Antonius Scriptor? Say rather Henoch ben Nethaneel, an agent of the proconsul. Accursed be his memory!"

The two guardsmen dragged the young man through the crowds. "Who is he? Who is he?" asked many voices.

"Who is it?" asked Menachem. A large, bearded fellow with a Northern Galilean accent replied: "Yesterday his name was still worth two hundred talents. No more; the Romans will bleed a few more urns of Jewish blood. He was nineteen and full of courage, Chanina ben Sabbatai. We called him Son of Iron: Ben Barzeel. They've gotten him, they've taken him away."

The tumult had reached Jesus and his companions and the people were shouting: "Yeshua, Yeshua, help him, save Ben Barzeel!"

But Jesus turned to a poor woman who was looked at him with pleading eyes:

"What is your wish, woman?"

"I am bleeding. I bleed twelve months of the year and I cannot conceive children."

"Is that why you touched the hem of my garment?"

"Forgive me Rabbi, forgive your servant!"

"Yeshua, help him, Ben Barzeel is being taken away!"

Yeshua looked the poor pilgrim woman in the eye: "Woman, your faith has saved you. You may go, the bleeding has ceased and you will bear children."

"Ben Barzeel, Yeshua, give Ben Barzeel back to us!"

Yeshua followed on. "Once again he has taken a step outside of Israel," thought Menachem. "While he could have himself crowned as King of Israel."

"O God, let me walk the way of eternity." That was Yeshua's wish but those following him did not understand. Menachem forced a path through the people to get close to Ben Barzeel. The young man appeared strong so the two police had to pull and push. They hit him on the head and back and kicked his legs.

"He is a follower of Ben Nesher," thought Menachem bitterly. "Even he has faith, Yeshua! He is as worthy as the woman who bled. He also has a mother and a father that will mourn. If his belief in Israel is not sacred then neither the Law nor the prophets are sacred, then Sinai is not sacred, God is not holy and your calling is not sacred. Then all the links are loose and there's no beginning."

Then Menachem cried out at the risk of being arrested: "And you, many thousands, let that happen to a man who acted on behalf of Israel!" Menachem had already drawn his knife to intervene but some men by his side grabbed his arm and held it against his side.

"The man deserves death," someone said. "You call him an avenger of Israel. This Zealot does not increase our freedom, he imperils it. Death to the ignorant fool. Our freedom is too precious to be risked like that."

"Freedom?" cried Menachem. "Where is our freedom?"

"Do we not bring offerings to the Temple and pray in the synagogue? That is our freedom. What more is there?"

"Who are you?" asked Menachem. His opponent was of short stature, with a high forehead. He had a thin, bent nose and large, black, passionate eyes. Everything about him spoke of zeal and fury. His arms and legs and his whole crouching body were prepared for action.

"Leave him alone Saul!" shouted a companion. "I know him, he is from Nazareth, a follower of Yeshua the deceiver."

"Who are you?" asked Menachem.

"I am Saul of Tarsus."

"He's a Nazarene of Jesus!"

"Nay, he's an Herodian. He wants to entrap us. If we had helped Barzeel, he would have delivered us up."

"Just look at his face. He's a smart gentleman. A well groomed noble! Beware, he's strong. He looks down on us. We are only poor, simple Jews. He's a Sadducee!"

"Have you finished yelling and cursing?" asked Menachem. "I am Menachem, a friend of Israel and will say this to you: Once there was a body that wanted to live. The legs said to the heart: 'work for us, why bother with the arms!' The arms said to the heart: 'Work for us, why bother with the legs!' The eyes said to the heart: 'give us blood, we want to see. Why bother with all the organs?' The heart replied: 'I want to beat for all of you' The legs, the arms and the eyes answered: 'Rather die then, than work for the others', so the heart died and also the legs, the arms and the eyes."

"Hail Menachem, that is so clever! Did you hear that from Yeshua, the great rabbi?"

"You are so strong in the Law," Menachem said to Saul of Tarsus, summing him up. "What have you against Ben Barzeel? Why may I not save him?"

"With his dagger he endangers the Law."

"And what did Moses do with the Egyptian? He brought him down since the Egyptian had done evil to an Israelite. Moses put Israel in danger. Yet this week you will honor Moses on the evening of Pesach. The Israelites of Moses' time spoke just like you and your friends, Saul of Tarsus. They told Moses who wanted to save them: 'Do you want to murder us too, like you did the Egyptian?' People don't want to take risks."

"You speak like Yeshua of Nazareth."

"Nay, I speak for Yeshua of Nazareth and for Ben Barzeel the Zealot and for you yourselves, Pharisees, and for all who mean well with Israel. In humility I say, 'I feel like the heart and all of you would rather kill me than save Israel with me.'"

"Let him be, he will suffer the same fate as Jesus, they will hang together!" said Saul of Tarsus with contempt.

2

Menachem had intended to visit the parents of the captured Zealot Ben Barzeel but he first wanted to see Yocheved and her mother. He had to change his clothes also as there were traitors amongst the masses, and some of them had noticed when he pulled the knife to avenge the Zealot. He thus avoided the crowds going up to the Temple by taking the road to Bet-Zetha.

Yocheved lived in the new city in the Avenue of Almond Trees. Meeting him in the street, she looked lovelier than ever with her full rosy cheeks.

"I've heard that you were here and that you had once again succumbed to your wild side. What's the point of living wisely and carefully for 29 days of the month only to do something foolish on the thirtieth?"

"That's what I save the twenty-nine days for, Yocheved. What other use is there for circumspection," he asked with a smile.

"Come, Menachem, Baruch has grown so you'll be able to speak to him. We have a child that was cast upon you from an unknown lap," she said bitterly.

"I know you still blame me for not having married you. How could I do that, Yocheved? Do you want to be the wife of a drifter who follows someone that he doesn't know the path of?"

"Israel?"

"Aye, Israel."

"Always Israel. My father has also returned home. There are some men with him and they speak about your friend Yeshua! Perhaps it would be good for you to join them."

Yocheved pushed Menachem ahead into a dark passage. She wished to accommodate her beloved in his most secret and profound longings. He was attached to Yeshua and she knew of his love for Israel. She was aware that he wanted to save each of them for the other. That's why she led him through the corridor and hid him behind a curtain outside the room in which the conversation took place.

First Menachem heard a familiar voice, the words of one who spoke with great urgency. He had seldom heard a more passionate voice in this land of spiritual zeal.

"It cannot carry on like this. He blasphemes and transgresses the Law. If we permit him to continue living in our midst, we are really begging God for our damnation."

"Saul is right!" another chimed in.

"He's telling the people that salvation is near while the nation totters on the edge of the abyss. We must apprehend Jesus and deliver him to the Romans! They will know what to do with him!"

"To deliver one Jew to the idolators," shouted Abba Alexander, "would be to blaspheme God's holy name."

"He is the blasphemer. He claims to be the son of God."

"Since when is that considered blasphemy in Israel?" asked the calm voice of Sirach. "Are we not all children of God?"

"You are distorting the truth, Sirach. He means that he is God's chosen son."

Menachem exclaimed: "Are we not God's chosen nation? Why should God not also have a chosen son amongst his chosen children?"

"Who's that?" asked Abba Alexander.

A momentary silence followed.

"He has said that he is above the Law and above the Sabbath!" shouted the companion of Saul of Tarsus. "Is that not enough for you? I say the man must die! Would you rather that the Law in us perish along with God's glory in his world?"

"We could call him before the Sanhedrin and request of him to explain his teaching in greater detail," suggested an older voice.

"He won't come, the sly fox, he feels safest when he is surrounded by the people."

"We must arrest him and deliver him to the Romans. He is inciting the people against Caesar and his order. We will pay the price for that!"

"Chilul HaShem, Chilul HaShem!"[1] many voices responded.

"But if it becomes necessary, would it not be better to give up one man to save the many? If we hand him to the Romans, the proconsul will regard it as a gesture of goodwill. Even if he is innocent, one man can suffer on behalf of the others."

---

1. Profaning God's name.

"That's an affront to God," cried Abba Alexander. "That is the way of the nations!"

"There may not be injustice in Israel, Jews!" Menachem appeared from behind the curtain. "Israel may not sin like this!"

"The son of the merchant!"

"Where's your father Menachem?" asked one of the men in a mocking tone. "Still in Syria with the foreign woman? Is Rachel still weeping about the divorce papers he sent her?"

"If you do not shut up I will silence you with a blow!" Sirach shouted at the man who was mocking Menachem.

Menachem continued: "Men, I tell you, should the devil give you the choice: 'Choose either the well-being of the nation and the land—and commit one injustice—or commit no injustice but perish,' then it would be Israel's duty to commit no injustice. Amongst the nations the interest of the many may outweigh justice for one but not in Israel. Thus we learnt from our Prophets. King Ahab was cursed. He may have extended the borders of Israel but he took a man's life for a piece of land. Jews, do not lay a hand on my friend Yeshua. It is his deepest wish that you do not lay your hands upon him but he will do everything so that you indeed do it. Yeshua must follow his path. Overcome him through love and understanding. If you do that, God will bless you and remove from him the burden that he intends to carry only because he feels he has to."

"That sounds like the schools of Alexandria!" someone cried.

"Men, save Yeshua and yourselves! The gazelle is sleeping, but to her left and right, in front and behind her, the traps are set. Yeshua has set you a trap, the Romans have set you a trap, God himself has set you a trap. Oh my Israel, my fast gazelle, do not move, for one moment do not move. Jacob wrestled with the angel one whole night long before he could move on. Do not move. In your passivity you will be blessed!"

"Those are mysterious words that I do not understand and have never read," said Abba Alexander. "Maybe the son of Marcus Mercator understands himself. We must remain vigilant, warning the people against the sophistries of Yeshua of Nazareth. However, what is in Israel must remain in Israel. May God strike him if he blasphemes. We cannot do that."

"And what do the wise say about the one that denies God?" cried the future Paul.

"He denies not the existence of God," replied Abba Alexander. "He is an excitable young man who has dreamt too much and imagines that he has a right to the Name."

"He preaches humility," said Nicodemus.

"Good! Our teachers do that too," Abba answered. "But does he set an example? I have never seen someone prouder than him."

"You are divided, as always, upholders of the honor of God," spat Saul of Tarsus with disdain. "I know you. When it comes down to it, the blood of one person will be of greater worth to you believers than God's word."

Another silence followed.

"If the elders would not dare anymore, we will act," cried one of Saul's companions.

"I want to ask you one question," Saul resumed. "Where is it written that Messiah is the son of God who was, is and shall be?"

Some elders shook their heads, others closed their ears.

"This Jesus follows in the footsteps of Isaiah but then he goes further! He tells the people that he works for the glory of God but I tell you he only thinks of his own glory. He claims to be the son of the Father but he dethrones the Father and knows better than what his Father taught us through Moses. He robs the nation of their belief in the Torah. A thief like Barabbas who was caught yesterday, steals less than him."

The men who were listening to Saul remained silent. Saul came from outside the land; young, new to the Law and more offended by Jesus than the elder Pharisees who were merely disturbed by events.

"There was a rock-hard mountain," said Menachem. "One man came to break the stone. He had his father's axe. The mountain did not split. Then with a sigh, he dropped his father's axe and took up a larger one. The mountain did not split. Then he took up such a massive axe that the handle was larger than himself. Please try to understand.

Prophet! Messiah! God's own son! Yeshua must wield a tool to open up humanity to God."

"Is the Law not sufficient?" cried Abba Alexander.

"The Law comes from Israel. The peoples do not want to be taught by a nation since that would humiliate them. We are sending Yeshua and we do not realize it," replied Menachem.

"Is Yeshua then a renegade, does he not care about Israel?"

"Yeshua is as natural to Israel as a fish in water. God himself has pulled him from his people. He does not know it and he does not want it."

"Israel, Israel, what do I have to do with Israel?!" Saul of Tarsus exploded in fury. "What is a nation of flesh and blood? It is about God's Holy Law! May Israel perish if it is not worth the Law and let a new Israel accept and cherish it."

"You too, Saul," said Menachem sadly. "You too do not care about Israel."

"Now we know what we're dealing with, idle talkers," shouted another young man. "You do nothing and will do nothing. You'll lie underneath the problem and look up to it with your tongue out of your mouth like dogs under the table. You deliberately refuse to understand in order to avoid taking action. We will act. We know someone who will help us and deliver Jesus up to us."

Menachem froze.

"His blood is upon us."

"Do not curse yourself," Menachem thundered. "You are too frail to bear blood guilt. One may only kill someone who has caused people grave harm. Yeshua means well for the people. He has healed and comforted so many! One may not kill his brother, not even on God's behalf. God does not want us to kill for him. Did he not save Isaac? Beware, beware of shedding blood in the name of God!"

"The son of Marcus Mercator does not plead for nothing. What is the Nazarene paying you?"

Menachem, devastated by what he had heard, turned and left.

"Did you hear?" he asked Yocheved who grabbed him by the arm.

"Aye."

"They are planning a double murder, on Jesus and on Israel. I'm going, I must save him."

3

Jerusalem was filled with people feverishly preparing to celebrate Pesach. The sages taught that every generation had to celebrate the exodus from Egypt as if they were experiencing it themselves. But it wasn't necessary to teach that anymore since each generation felt it every year. The people yearned for Pesach like one longs for the son, the sea and freedom. Around and inside Jerusalem there was no rest but a fever instead. So much cleaning had to be done. Sacrificial animals were already being prepared. People asked one another, "when will the Pesach of all Pesachs come, when will freedom be established forever?"

Menachem was looking for Jesus and his disciples amongst all this activity. However, Jesus knew that a plot was being hatched against him and was on his way to the town of his friend Lazarus where he would be safe.

They camped on the way when evening fell since Jesus did not wish to disturb his friends at this late hour. With his heart, he never liked the people, neither with his mind. He loved them with his will. They were lost and that is why he was sent. He didn't believe that he was a human being anymore. He looked at people with strange eyes. He had lived amongst them and now he was going away. He loved God only and now he was on his way to God. If you long for death, is it not childish to recoil from the manner in which the Father calls you home?

At the thought of the cross, Jesus was reminded of the people again—it wasn't true that he didn't like them. Although he didn't live with them, he lived amongst them for a long, long time. By now he knew too much about their problems to forget them. He chose people and one also comes to love those who serve you—Peter, John, Thomas, the nasty Judas. "I was never a child when I was young but now I remember how it was to be a child. I love children and enjoy it when they come to me. I do not know what I am; it is difficult to choose between heaven and earth, Father."

The night was pitch black since clouds obscured the stars. His disciples slept uneasily. Simon Peter got up. This night was unbearably heavy. It must have been like this for the Egyptians on the night of Pesach when they lost their firstborn.

Peter walked towards the bushy hill. "Simon Peter, Simon Peter," someone whispered. He got a fright; who was calling his name in the darkness?

"Simon Peter, listen to me!"

"I know that voice—is it you, unbeliever?"

"Yes, it's Menachem."

"What do I have to do with you? Don't touch me, witness who refuses to witness!"

"That's what you say. Why don't you rather say: a witness that refuses to give false witness? Simon Peter, you must listen to me. Do you love Yeshua?"

"Shut up! I do not speak with you about Jesus who is the Christ."

"They want to arrest and hand him over to the Romans who will crucify him."

"Dog, you are expressing your own desire."

"Do you really believe that Peter? I've known Yeshua much longer than you have. He did not choose me. I have followed him and I wish him well."

"You blaspheme. You don't believe in him!"

"Who is he, Peter?"

"I am not allowed to divulge that."

"I am. He is a human being. Adam was created, Jesus is a man."

"He is Mosheach, God's own son."

"Simon Peter, do you love Israel?"

"My nation is my life, you know that. My people are my life and Yeshua is the hand of God."

"If you love Israel, you must save Yeshua. Israel cannot afford to lose him.

I tell you, there's a plot to arrest him. One of your number is part of it."

"Who?"

Menachem held back. He imagined Jesus standing behind him, closing his mouth.

"I don't know. One of you but which one, I don't know. Please tell Yeshua to move away, to Perea, Arabia or Sidon, far away from here. Else the circle will be closed."

"Which circle?"

"That of the two halves: Israel and Yeshua. The nations will afflict Israel on Yeshua's behalf and afflict Yeshua on Israel's behalf. Please believe me, Simon Peter. I have acknowledged Jesus in my own way and he loves me. Please go before it's too late and I have to move away with Israel."

"Again you speak in riddles, faithless one."

"But not without loyalty. Warn him, Simon Peter . . ."

"And if Satan speaks through you?"

"Your Master once said: 'Would Satan ruin his own work? Is Satan against himself?'"

"I will go and warn him, Menachem."

That same night Menachem sneaked into his mother's house. He found her fully dressed but sleeping. He softly touched her, "Mother." She was with him immediately as she had fallen asleep thinking of him.

"I was waiting for you, Menachem."

She got up, embraced him and burst out in tears. "They were looking for you here."

"Who, mother?"

"The soldiers of the oppressor."

"I've just come to change clothes, Mother, then I'm off again."

"Menachem, I'm afraid for your friend Yeshua too."

"I understand that, Mother."

"You are staying with Israel but he's leaving us. When he entered the city on the little donkey, I was there in the crowds. People speak ill of him but he is your friend. I am aware that he acted unjustly towards many good, pious men. I know he wishes to do away with the plant to save the flower. And how fragrant is the flower that he offers—I have heard him speak!"

"He has no choice, mother. He has to leave the nation. Outside they do not recognize the plant as the flower is all. I have heard that a foreign woman asked him for the crumbs of his words. She was from Sidon. The nations are famished."

Menachem was quiet for a while. Then he exclaimed: "O mother, I am afraid that I won't be able to save Yeshua. Many a night I've dreamt about what will happen. Israel is the light of God but the nations cannot see that since Israel consists of ordinary sinful people. Ordinary people will not let themselves be instructed by other ordinary people. That's why Israel must let go of a piece of its light, a piece to be hurled high above the nations. Yeshua is not a nation, he is but one man. Nations will believe in him and he will teach them so that they do not feel humiliated. Since he lived on earth they will be able to worship a human being in the image of God. I call him the Son of Israel. It breaks my heart that Yeshua has not come to save Israel, now that our people are in such dire straits.

At this moment Israel needs deeds more than words as it is already filled with the food of God.

But Yeshua is looking for souls: empty souls, sinners and strangers. God will split the light in two but these will remain the twins of his mystery. And those who see the lights will know that they are brothers. That is what I have dreamt. Yet I must try to save him—there is still time."

"Go, my son. Adonai yevarechecha veyismerecha. May God bless you and keep you!" Rachel laid her hands on the head of her son.

4

ABBA ALEXANDER HAD KNOWN for a long time that his wife was unfaithful but never said anything. Wrongheaded friends wished to defend his honor and force him to face the facts. The law required two witnesses. So it happened that two witnesses caught Bathsheba with her lover, Valerius Pontus alias Natronai ben Ahitopel. However, when they entered Abba's room with the news of what was taking place in another room, the old man refused to accompany them in order to see his wife's humiliation. They then asked Abba what was to be done. "I first need to find an applicable document. Wait for me here." Unfortunately there were others who noticed the belligerent witnesses enter Abba's house and hoping for a scandal, were lingering about the gate. They saw the old Pharisee, who didn't want to become involved as a judge in his wife's fornication, sneak out through a side door. Some troublemakers pursued him, and grabbing him by the arm, loudly mocked the old man:

"So what are they going to do with her, Rabbi? Execute her?"

Abba Alexander struggled to breathe.

"What's the verdict, Pharisee, pious of the pious, are they going to kill her or not?"

He took a deep breath.

"So tell us, Law Expert!"

He groaned: "No, no, no!"

"Is that the Law or does the Law not apply to old Pharisees?"

Abba Alexander wiped the sweat from his brow. "Don't kill her, don't kill her . . . you would commit a great sin. She was only—a sob escaped the old, strict face—my concubine, an 'eshet pilegesh.'"

The men snickered.

"Old fraud, hypocrite who teaches others! He applies the Law to us, to the poor!"

The heavy old man wished to flee but couldn't escape them. The avengers followed and mocked him. Suddenly he stood still and called to them: "I lied. She's guilty, but I plead for mercy. It is written: 'God is a merciful God and the children of Israel are merciful and children of the merciful!'"

"Be still, for she didn't only sin against you Abba but against the whole nation. She has betrayed all of us. Death must follow," shouted one young fanatic who had joined the accusers. Abba Alexander's head began to spin

He heard the cry "Menachem, Menachem," from afar. Yocheved approached him and threw her arms around his neck. "Save my mother, Menachem, she's being humiliated in public. They've pulled her from the house."

Menachem put his arm around her shoulder and together they ran down the streets to the Nicanor Gate on the eastern side of the temple area.

Yocheved's mother Batsheba stood there in a white garment, surrounded by a jeering and hollering crowd. Her black hair sharply contrasted with the white of her breasts; she only managed to throw a small dark cloth over her shoulders before they pulled her away. The lover with whom she was caught had disappeared. A lamb sticks close to the ewe when she is attacked, a ram challenges the attacker, but the guilty wolf runs away.

The men surrounding Batsheba hurled rude insults at her as did the women who called her ugly names. Batsheba winced and placed her hands over her eyes but a young man pulled them away. When upstanding people surround a sinner, a transfer takes place which reveals that the sinner is cleaner than them. One man gave Batsheba a terrible blow on the hip. She screamed in pain. She stood there cornered like a doe.

"Stone her, stone her now!" the men shouted. "That'll drown her passion!" women shrieked.

"She's already suffered so much, she'll die even before they do it," thought Menachem.

"Help her, she's my mother!" Yocheved begged him as her life seemed to drain from her.

"What can I do, Yocheved, I have no authority!"

At that moment a company of men descending from the Mount of Olives appeared on the scene. The tumult immediately died down.

Recognizing Jesus of Nazareth, the pious expected an interesting encounter, as they were the types whose questions were always aimed at measuring his adherence to the Law.

Scattered voices were still heard: "Stone her, stone her!"

The young scribe Mathias bar Yochai, one of the avengers of Abba's honor, stopped Jesus. As the crowd stood back Batsheba gained some relief. One could see it in her breathing.

"Rabbi," said Mathias, "this woman was caught in the act of adultery in the view of two witnesses. What must we do with her? It is written: 'lo tinuf—you will not commit adultery.' The people are outraged; they want justice. It is written: 'When a man commits adultery with a married woman, the adulteress and the man who committed it with her must be executed.' What do you say of this?"

An expectant silence fell as Jesus had earned great respect amongst the people.

Mathias bar Yochai seemed to take the matter very seriously. Jesus did not or he didn't seem to take Mathias bar Yochai seriously or he was searching for another truth. Bending down, he wrote something with his finger in the dust on the street. This gave Batsheba some hope.

Then Jesus stood up, looking at the young Mathias and the members of the crowd who stared at him in anticipation, some still holding stones.

A mixture of mockery and seriousness shone in his eyes. He was weighing the nature of man.

Slowly he replied: "The one amongst you who has no sin may throw the first stone."

Immediately the harshest men and the most outspoken women dropped their stones. Batsheba screamed. Those who had encircled her dispersed, including the scribes.

Looking at Batsheba with the little cloth barely covering her naked shoulders, Jesus said: "Woman, where are those who accused you now? Did nobody dare to condemn you?" She shyly glanced at him. She didn't know why he had saved her life.

"Nobody sir," she replied.

Then Jesus continued: "I don't either. I do not condemn you. Go on your way and sin no more."

Batsheba, who had not even noticed the presence of her daughter and Menachem in the crowd of accusers, stood there against the temple gate. Although not inflicted by stones, her wound was deeper than she realized. She staggered home.

Then Yocheved spoke as if she had made a choice: "I will follow your friend" and let go of Menachem's hand to follow after Jesus.

Menachem waited a day before visiting the home of Abba Alexander in the Lane of Almond Trees. The servants told him that Yocheved was out, so he headed to the living room, the triclinium. The world-weary old man on the sofa looked up as Menachem entered.

It was Abba Alexander but the serious, strict old Pharisee was broken.

"Come in, Menachem, make yourself at home," he said in a weak voice. "You're with someone who has broken his sword."

"What's wrong, Abba Alexander? Are you not a warrior of the Law anymore?"

The old man sighed. "I cannot lift my hand against the man that claims that he is above the Law. I cannot raise my voice against Jesus of Nazareth anymore. He has saved my wife. Rabbi Hillel emphasized the mercy of God. Therefore I have to believe that God speaks through Yeshua. Yes, he does and says things that I disapprove of but have I the right to judge the savior of my wife, Menachem? Times are difficult.

My whole life I devoted to God's Law but I have kept quiet about God. I have loved him."

Menachem mumbled: "My friend Yeshua contradicts himself. He needs the teachers of religion just like the Law needs its legal experts."

Not listening to Menachem, Abba Alexander sighed: "I want to be reconciled with my wife and forgive her. She refuses, Menachem," he sighed again.

Menachem doubted that the infatuated woman would come to her senses. And why should he have empathy with her? She does not reciprocate.

"I've tried to follow Yeshua's advice to be kind towards her. Yeshua spoke to her like a good Jew. Do you know how she responded when I mentioned the one who saved her? 'He didn't save me! He told me not to sin again.' And Batsheba went further: 'My sin is what saves me. Why did he give me my life only to take it away again?' Is that not evil and ungrateful?"

"Where is Yocheved?" asked Menachem.

"She'll be here some time. Every day now she looks for Yeshua of Nazareth to hear his words."

Suddenly the old man was seized with anguish: "Oh Menachem, I am old and perhaps I am dumb. But I have served God and Israel with my whole heart. Now I do not mind passing on. My wife and daughter have accused me of giving them no place in their hearts, saying that I only thought of the Torah. But the Law is the abode of God, all that we have of God on earth. They do not realize that I always took them with me."

Menachem had an idea. "May I speak to Batsheba?"

Abba Alexander gestured with his hand. Walking down various passages, Menachem reached a fragrant woman's apartment. Batsheba was lying on a divan, weeping inconsolably.

"Batsheba!"

She looked up. "What do you want?"

"Why are you crying?"

"Why I weep? Go ask Yeshua your friend. Is he the Messiah? If so, ask him to take away the sin or dismiss the command against the sin!"

She got up and shouted: "I'm in anguish. I yearn for my friend. And the pain here and here and here—she pointed to her heart, her breasts and her head—are worse than the pain that the stones would have inflicted. Yeshua told me not to sin again but I am a sinner, I sin, I live for sin! Let him remove it from me or raise his hand and say: 'That is no sin. Go, woman, and be happy.'"

"Batsheba, do you have any feeling for your husband? He is old and downhearted."

"Am I Abishag and is he David?"

"You are hurting him with your sin. The real sin is causing hurt."

"Look at yourself, preacher! You are young and handsome. Look what you're doing to my daughter by not sinning with her. You are killing her. Believe me, those people who resist sin cause more hurt on earth than the sinners. Go and tell that to your friend Yeshua."

At that moment Yocheved appeared, noting with displeasure how her mother was showering Menachem with accusations.

"Where were you?" she asked Yocheved.

"With my Messiah. He wanted to save you but he found your daughter."

"My Messiah," sighed Menachem, bowed to Batsheba and touched the hand of Yocheved. "Now Yocheved has her own Messiah!" and he left.

5

THE FEVER OF PASSOVER had taken hold of the city. Strong passions pulsated through the air as people made haste to pull time towards them like a rope; this was the time of breaking down and building up.

Jesus reminded himself that his days were nearing their end. He did not live his own life and it seemed to him that he only existed to observe and to witness. Time was up. But in his soul there remained a core of earthly life which caused him pain.

The most mortal part of him did not wish to die. He was leaving much behind because he had come to love many. "My Father, you have sent me over the world like a whirlwind but somewhere along the line I became a tree that struck root. It pains me that I have to die but that is your will. And what else could I still do for you?"

The apostles were quiet; they sensed the reflective mood of their Master. In the town of Bethany they came to the tomb of the prophet Zechariah. Lazarus, of whom people said that he was raised from the dead by the prophet after four days in the grave, lived in the town with his sisters Mariam and Martha. All three were of the same generation as Yeshua. The arrival of their Master was cause for great joy. Even in his absence they lived for and through him.

Jesus rested with them because they were simple people who needed no persuasion or miracles anymore. There was much joy in the reunion.

Large white tables had been set up in the small house of Lazarus. Jesus rested and some of his companions were so exhausted from the heat and hunger that they fell asleep.

The busy Martha, mistress of the household, laid bread in front of the men. She brought the salt and, assisted by a servant girl, wooden dishes filled with fish. The apostles ate with relish.

It was the eve of Sabbath. Simon Peter and Matthew Levi took up a psalm as the sky emptied of light.

"Where is Mariam?" Yeshua asked Lazarus whose real name was Eliazar. "Here she comes." Younger than Martha, Mariam with her large black eyes was totally devoted to Yeshua and had declined two marriage proposals on that account. She carried a jar filled with ointment of which the fragrance filled the whole house.

She knelt in front of Yeshua, took some ointment and anointed his feet. Then she took her hair in her hands and rubbed the ointment into the skin of his feet with this symbol of her beauty. The apostles did not approve. This sort of thing happened in the homes of Romans and the rich Sadducees of Jerusalem. Noticing their discomfort, Judas hoped to take advantage of the situation. He seldom had the chance to speak for others and it gave him great satisfaction: "Is that not a great sin? Do you know what the ointment costs? Three hundred dinar at today's prices! Just think how many of the poor we could have fed with that amount."

The Master looked up while laying a hand on Mariam's black hair that smelled like a field of wild flowers at night. In a melancholic voice he said: "Leave her be as I will not be with you much longer while you will always have the poor. You bought this ointment for my grave, didn't you Mariam?"

The company was gripped by fear, except Judas who smiled knowingly. He had gotten used to the idea of Yeshua's early death and considered himself a collaborator of Yeshua as well as of those who wanted to kill him.

"What can I still do to prevent it, what can I do to avoid it?" Menachem asked himself over and over, night and day. He now wore a beard and was dressed like one of the Essenes who knew the secrets of healing. In Jerusalem he searched for Mathias bar Yochai and Saul of Tarsus. Finally he visited Sirach, his mother's friend, whose mournful face disturbed him. "What's wrong, Sirach?"

"My son has joined the Nazarenes."

"And that pains you? I thought that you found much truth in the words of Yeshua?"

"You know my opinion, Menachem. It cannot be. When the idolators get grapes from us, they become stones in their hands—stones they cast at us. My son is part of that now."

"Sirach, night comes on. I've heard that a group of Pharisees is hatching a plot against Yeshua!"

Sirach knew: "What is the accusation? He serves God. He claims to be the Son of God. It might be literal; it might be meant as metaphor. That is

God's secret. What is his quarrel with the Pharisees? He seeks them out to confront them. Why does he ignore those who have become Greek and the collaborators of the Romans?"

"People seek their opponents amongst their kin," replied Menachem.

"You're right. Yeshua is a subversive Pharisee, Menachem; there's absolutely no common ground between him and the Epikurim[1] who have embraced Greek culture. That is why he never bothers with them."

"Do you know where his enemies are gathering?"

"Cover your face, Menachem so they do not recognize you, and we'll go there together."

They proceeded towards the vicinity of the Temple. Evening was settling on the city. On Birkat Israim Square they observed a group of men who had just started moving so the two of them fell in with this group. To Menachem's surprise, the destination was the home of the high priest . . .

"They are even collaborating with Sadducees to defeat Yeshua," he whispered to Sirach. "Those who lack respect for the Law are joining up with those who lack power."

The conspirators entered the palace through a humble doorway. Menachem waited outside while Sirach entered. After about an hour a familiar figure approached. He grabbed the man's arm and said: "It's you, Judas, I knew it."

Judas snickered.

"You observed well, unbeliever, it is I."

"So you intend to deliver your Master to the enemy?"

"Nothing of the sort. I only want the pious to fall into sin up to their necks. When I was a young man, they would not allow me to speak in their meetings. I first had to study in order to earn the right to speak. When I became a man, I was not allowed to earn a little interest on the small amount of money that my father had left me. I had to take a job as shoe-maker with a rabbi. Women were too expensive or ugly to me but the rabbi insisted that a Jew had to get married. My whole life they harassed me. And now they themselves are falling into sin."

"You are betraying your Master for that?"

"Unbelievers never understand anything. The rabbis want me to do this. Even in the Law there's not much fun in having to pray always. God is monotonous. They want to hate too. And my Master wants to put an end to

---

1. General Jewish term for apostates, probably referring to the pleasure-seeking goals of the Greek Epicurean school of philosophy.

it all—there's no other way out for him. He simply cannot do all that he has promised. He cannot make all of us happy. Don't you see, I have to do this job for him at the cost of my eternal damnation. Whether it be the rabbis or Jesus of Nazareth, they all want to enter the Kingdom of God. And guess what the key is? The sinner! Saving sinners or making sinners—as long as there's a sinner to use." He snickered again. "That is why my Master is so concerned with sinners. They are the key for those brave people who want to enter God's Kingdom."

"Judas, Judas, what has happened between you and Yeshua?"

"I'm angry with him."

"Do you not love him anymore?"

"How dare you speak like that, unbeliever? He is worth more than all of you. But I am cross with him."

"Why?"

"I will tell you, sweet-talking scoundrel. He creates us."

"But you existed before you knew him."

"He creates us by foretelling what we will do. He has foreknowledge. And what can we do about it? We are compelled to do what he has predicted."

"A disciple must obey his Master, Judas."

"Yes but hold it a minute. Jesus predicted that we would do bad things. Then we do it. Is that obedience, unbeliever?"

"That is also obedience."

"You asked if I liked Yeshua. I am not sure anymore."

"Why not?"

"He wants to use me for the dirty work. He despises me. First he made me the treasurer and in our circle we despise money. They will all despise me even more, unbeliever, because now he wants . . ."

"What?"

"Why should I not tell you? He wants me to betray him. That is why he chose me in the first place. All the others were chosen for the Kingdom of Heaven."

Judas started sobbing; his sobs resembled his snickers except they were more frightening. One was tempted to smash his skull instead of comforting him.

"Do you understand, unbeliever? Simon Peter must be blessed for his sake—and I must be condemned. You will see, he grants no one any self-respect. What a nice word. He did bless Simon Peter but he brought him to his knees and he made him sin. He loves the sin that humiliates mankind as much as the rabbis love an extension to the Law."

Judas was convulsed by an attack of the snickers so wild that he looked like a braying donkey to Menachem.

"God let Moses sin," Menachem said cautiously.

"Jesus said things against Simon Peter that, well, if he had said it to me, no matter how I loved him, I would have . . ."

"Betrayed him."

"I did not say that. It has nothing to do with you. Die, dog. I'm not even allowed to speak to you. My Master dislikes you."

Judas sped away, vanishing into one of Jerusalem's little alleyways in which it was difficult to follow someone.

The day before Passover, Menachem had the idea to kill Judas before it was too late. Neither Yeshua nor the group of conspirators could be stopped now. They both believed they were acting for the good.

But Judas was guilty because he knew he was betraying an innocent man. Should Menachem kill Judas, disaster might still be averted. So he searched high and low and found him at sunset in the company of a few others near the palace of the high priest. The palace was situated in the southwest of the city; its roof provided a view of the eerie Valley of Gehennom in all its morbid gloom.

The other men entered the palace of Caiaphas while Judas headed towards the inner city. The Feast of Liberation was near and under no circumstances would Judas miss the communal meal at the side of Yeshua.

Judas was walking briskly down the street of the coppersmiths, followed by Menachem with his hand on his dagger. As he caught up with him, Menachem lifted his dagger when his felt his hand being restrained from behind; it was Jesus in the spirit.

"Menachem, leave Judas Iscariot alone, he is doing my will," Jesus said in a loud, clear voice. "Will we leave the nations without a God?"

"We are chosen for sacrifice," replied Menachem.

He rubbed his eyes; Jesus had disappeared. He took a deep breath and lowered his arm. Judas never knew that his life was spared by two good men, obedient ones, two men of Israel that were resigned to the election of Israel.

Later that night Menachem experienced a strange vision. Peter spoke to him: "I will do it, Menachem. I have promised you that I will prevent Yeshua from sacrificing his flesh. I will keep my promise." Then Menachem saw Yeshua surrounded by his disciples. He was saying to them: "I came to Jerusalem to die but I will live again on the third day." Shocked, Peter grabbed his arm, saying: "Do not say that, Master! That will not happen! You will live and keep teaching us. We cannot survive without you!"

The normally calm and peaceful Yeshua reacted in fury: "Go away from me, Satan, you are a stumbling stone to me. You are not inspired by God." Then Peter fell on his knees in front of Yeshua and begged forgiveness. Menachem heard his own voice: "Yeshua, are you so afraid of human words, of the words of friends, that you honestly think that the devil has entered into Peter? Now I know you wish to die in order not to know that you also wish to live. You prefer divinity to humanity because when someone loves his brothers as much as you love them, there is no other way of escape. Nothing will persuade you otherwise. If it is written that Mosheach has to die in order to live again, change the Scripture that you say you came to fulfill. I beg you in the name of Israel not to do it; your death will bring calamity to your people. Light of the light of the chosen, remain in the light of your people. Yet I know that my plea will achieve nothing as the time is ripe and in the fullness of time we discern His will."

After the feverish preparation, peace descended on the evening of Pesach. Menachem wanted to celebrate it with so many people. Amongst them were the parents of the Zealot Ben Barzeel. In one of the city's poorest districts he found their house. Around the Passover meal a man, woman and girl lay on cushions.

"We have no joy yet we celebrate," he said.

"Sit and eat with us, stranger."

"Why is there no joy here?"

"The Romans arrested and killed our only son."

"I know, he was my friend, a follower of Ben Nesher, and Ben Nesher was my friend."

"People claim that he was a rebel," said the man, "that he put us all in danger. He rose up against the Romans and one is not allowed to do that."

"He was our only son," sighed the mother. "What is there left for a mother on earth?" She started crying silently. The girl said: "My brother has gone. I was so proud of him. He was big and strong and my friends looked at him with admiring eyes. My brother was my pride. I was Miriam and he was Moses. Now I'll never see him again."

"Did you come to see our grief, stranger?" asked the man.

"Your son will have children in Israel," declared Menachem with conviction. "Wonders will happen. One century will be without him but in the next, his seed will rise again and he will have children in Israel. We may be just simple Jews but Israel is an exalted ark. We do not know who carries it but there must be many. In one of the columns on which Israel rests I perceive my friend Ben Nesher and my comrade Ben Barzeel. Take comfort mother and sister, take comfort father, your son is with us and remains amongst us."

Then he also sat down and ate matzos and drank of the wine. After the second jug he greeted them and went on to the house of Sirach. Sirach was a rich man from Jericho and his house in Jerusalem was impressive. The Passover meal was spread upon a long table: cakes of unleavened bread, bitter herbs, mutton of the lamb, fruits and wine in vases. At the head of the table was Sirach while his wife Rivkah, daughters Chavah and Milkah, his young son Anan and two educated men were spread around the sides. They were discussing the meaning of the Exodus.

"Now we are slaves again in our own land," sighed Rivkah.

"It is claimed that we move from slavery to freedom," said Sirach. "But we move from freedom through slavery into freedom—there are three beats to the rhythm. And remember friends—God is always ahead of us. Abraham was still in Ur when God was already in the land; No matter how profound our grief, it is only because we are behind the joy that is meant for us." But despite his optimistic words, Sirach sighed deeply. The girl Milkah started crying.

"What's the matter, Sirach, why are you sighing on Passover?" asked Menachem as he entered.

"Have something to eat, Menachem. Have you left your mother alone tonight?"

"I will go to my mother shortly," replied Menachem. He was struck by the sad faces around the table.

"What's wrong, Sirach?"

"My son is not with us—the first Passover that he's not here."

"Where is he?"

"He wanted to be with the Nazarene, he said. He said that eating the bread and drinking the wine near Yeshua would make him the richest man alive."

"And you are sad about that?"

"His place is here; I am old, Menachem. He was on the path of my fathers but now I am alone again. What is someone worth to himself?"

"Your son has chosen a good way, Sirach!"

"Do you believe that, Menachem? It's a way that leads out of Israel. It is written that the nations would be blessed through us. That would be impossible without losing some of our children. Children that follow Yeshua are like drops of Israel's blood . . ."

"Lost to Israel!"

"Lost to Israel but they will flourish amongst the nations. It is hard to lose children but why were we chosen? Only for our own sake? We are a nation of strong men and fertile women. We were chosen to give and to sacrifice. A people of priests. This is a time of bleeding, Menachem. Jewish blood is being applied to the doorposts of the nations."

"They will not be grateful," sighed Rivkah.

"Be comforted Sirach! Israel is like Jerusalem. There will always be roads leading away from and towards it. The son of Sirach is leaving, the son of the emigrant merchant Marcus Mercator stays. The ways of eternity must be taken."

Menachem ate and drank but he felt unhappy, as if his words were hollow. They were meant to comfort.

In Jesus parents were losing their children. It was a time of giving birth and of the bleeding of the spirit. He stood up and thanked them before leaving. Darkness had fallen—the stars pierced the black veil of night with sharp light.

Menachem was looking for Jesus. He was convinced that a new Passover was being celebrated there, a Pesach outside of Israel. He recognized some followers of Yeshua in the street of the leather workers north of the Temple area, so he followed them. They were heading for a large house from which every now and then a man would emerge to stare into the darkness. Must be one of the disciples.

He entered the garden and hid himself when the two disciples Matthew Levi and Yochanan emerged briefly, then re-entered the house. He reached a palm tree at a corner of the house and climbed it to reach the roof and found a small hole through which he could see the large room below.

The twelve disciples that Jesus had chosen to represent the tribes of Israel were there.

Jesus looked sad and worried. Menachem thought that Jesus had always looked preoccupied, never happy nor sad. Now he looked sad. "Our land will be empty without Yeshua. Why does he not want to be a human being? Or is it me that insists he is a man when he is not? Who knows?"

Then Yeshua started to speak beautifully and tenderly like a human being, telling his disciples; "My children, I will not be with you for much longer. So I want to teach you a new mitzvah, a new commandment. Love one another like I loved you. There is no greater love than giving one's life for one's friends. I do not call you my servants anymore but my friends."

The disciples bowed their heads.

"I chose you; you didn't choose me," Yeshua continued, whereupon Menachem recalled that the same happened with Moses, Saul and David. But Abraham and Noah had chosen God and the mutual love was no less profound on account of that.

For the last time Menachem drank in the words of his friend whose humanity would bleed due to the twelve cuttings that he had planted—his twelve apostles. And to Menachem he remained a contradiction to the end. Still moved by the words "My children" with which Yeshua had addressed his followers, he heard him say: "No one comes to the Father except through me."

Without thinking, Menachem took hold of his knife. He saw it shining in the starlight before cutting open his cloak and whispering: "Sirach once said:

'The time is not yet right!' Woe to us and woe to Yeshua. It cannot be anymore.

When you came to open the door more widely, God spoke through you. Now when you said 'No one comes to the Father except through me...' I hear the voices of people. I cannot take part in this Passover meal."

Yeshua partook of the matzos and the wine . . . and prayed: "Baruch Atta Adonai boré peri ha-gafen. Blessed are you, our Lord, creator of the vine." When he handed matzos and wine to his disciples, he said: "This is my flesh, this is my blood." Menachem remembered Yeshua's terrible intention to sacrifice his own body and thought in desperation: "Yeshua, why do you want to do this?"

A voice inside answered: "For the sins of the people. But Yeshua, save your flesh and blood and eyes and mouth for your light and your word. Do you not know your own Father? God forgives our sins—our sacrifice is our suffering!"

He slid down the palm tree feeling exhausted and oblivious of his surroundings.

He prayed; "You made Jacob struggle with the angel. You sent Samuel to Saul. Send Yeshua to me. I want to struggle with him like a brother; I do not want him to be slaughtered."

And there Jesus stood in front of him. Menachem grabbed him by the legs.

"Yeshua, do not do it, do not go to the cross," he pleaded. "Flee away."

"And the people, Menachem, must they remain waiting?"

"Yeshua, God does not demand a sacrifice. The people desire a sacrifice and you demand it of yourself. If you had been able to do away with the sorrow of this generation and of those still to come, and if you could remove sin from this and future generations, would you still wish to die?"

"I must fulfill my destiny."

"You want to shed your despair by your blood on the cross—you despair over the evil of humanity and over your inability to help them."

"That is blasphemy, unbeliever. I bring hope to humanity."

"Yes, Yeshua, you'll give the people hope. But that hope is born of your despair."

"I ought to kill you now Menachem but there is no violence in me."

"You cannot kill me, Yeshua, since I know that you are in me and I in you, even if just for the moment. God has given you holiness for your path and for your words—do not waste them in order to become even holier."

Menachem let him go and Yeshua stood there, deep in thought.

"I must die, Menachem. I have to do it in order to make them believe."

"Do they only believe in blood, Yeshua? Do they only believe in their own unhappiness? Do they want God to bleed, do they love themselves so much that they wish to see God bleed like themselves? I cannot believe it, Yeshua, Yeshua!

I want to prevent the terrible suffering they want to inflict on you but I cannot. You however, will not achieve what you expect. I am telling you in truth, you will not sacrifice yourself for humanity but because of humanity. You want to die since you were unable to save this world with your life. You wish to die since you could not save mankind in the way you wished. You were not able to reconcile the contradictions!"

Jesus exclaimed: "You are cursed! You will wander like a stranger on earth for many, many centuries."

Menachem replied; "Yeshua my friend, please understand. In truth, I will wander all over, but you will be with me. You will see me suffer and it will hurt you since you are my friend and we move on the Way of Eternity. Oh Yeshua, my pain will be a sign of your ineffective work and your heart will contract with grief. Escape, because if you choose the cross, many crosses will be raised all over. And consider this: the people will say to their brothers whose suffering they observe: 'He has suffered more than you' and they will accept the suffering of their brethren with greater resignation. You will see it and you will be there just like I stay with my poor people Israel, like a mournful witness.

You will be with the people in the nations and hear their words of error; you will see that they extend the wrong hand to you just like they have done up to now to our Father. They are only human. You will admonish them: 'Mercy, mercy!' They will not understand and they will reply: 'We thank you Lord!'"

"Menachem, someone who speaks against me like this, I have to curse," said Jesus.

"You cannot curse me, Yeshua. I have already been cursed in the blessing of God. Woe is me, blessing is mine! I am Israel, Yeshua, just like you. Oh my friend, you are only one step away from our way of sorrow and your way of sorrow. We are united in the blessing that on earth looks like a curse."

Menachem took a few steps back, gave Jesus a loving glance and said: "You have overcome me Yeshua, since I know that you must overcome. Go! Be the sacrifice of Israel for them so the nations may think that Israel sacrificed you to herself, in order to draw even more of Israel's blood."

"Menachem, Menachem, keep my people Israel," Jesus pleaded tenderly.

"Who am I to do such a thing, Yeshua? Yet I will stay!"

"Follow the balanced path, Menachem, according to the Father's will!"

"Amen, Amen, Amen," exclaimed Menachem with conviction, "I believe, I believe, I believe, Yeshua. I believe in that which we both believe."

After this conversation Menachem fell asleep to awake after a few hours with the memory that he had to visit his mother.

6

Two mothers were searching for their sons. Yeshua's long absence had made Miriam distraught. Old and frail, her husband was unable to go up to Jerusalem. She had intended to celebrate the feast with him in Nazareth. She could not stop worrying about her son, however, and feared for his safety. In the somber mood of the nation she found the sign that persuaded her to observe the Passover in Jerusalem together with other pilgrims from Nazareth. She expected to find her son in the city. Galileans from all over assembled together to take the main road to the capital of Judea. Miriam looked youthful with her white veil, a light blue linen garment and simple wooden sandals. She remained a simple woman that only wished to love her son—she had no need of the fame he had brought her. In fact, she was hoping for the impossible.

Although his greatness made her happy, she would have wished for it to remain restricted to the household in Nazareth. Of course it could not; greatness had to be seen amongst the people so that they might be inspired to improve themselves. Yet in the same process greatness was broken down. Miriam appreciated the simple things and now people were making a fuss over her. When the people of Capernaum, Cana, Magdala, Gamala and Bethsaida arrived she noticed that a large group left their companions to join the caravan of Nazareth. She got a fright when it seemed as if they were all headed towards her. This fear was not without foundation—they were coming towards her, at least a thousand strong, it seemed. When they came near where she was sitting on the side of the road in the company of other women, they lifted their arms and chanted: "Blessed are you, Miriam, blessed among women and blessed is your womb!"

She blushed; these must be followers of Yeshua. What they said was kind and well-meant but it embarrassed her. She was a simple woman, the wife of Joseph the carpenter and she was blessed through her child. Why were the people saying these things in such a strange manner? Why not instead approach and say: "Shalom Miriam, to you and your son. We love him very much." Then she would have spoken to them, replying: "Shalom to you Chanina and to you Abba and to you Chanan, Joseph, Baruch, Nachum and you, my sisters Elizabeth, Rivkah, Deborah, Shulamit and Sarah, peace to all of you and thank you for loving my son."

She felt moved but not happy. The Nazareth caravan began to move, finding itself next to a group of people from Sepphoris amongst whom Miriam had some childhood acquaintances. She recognized Shoshanah the wife of Otniel the saddle maker.

"Peace to you, Shoshana!" Miriam called, always pleased to see a familiar face. There was no reaction and a whole queue of people turned their faces away. Amongst these was Rabbi Micha ben Chanina in whose yard Miriam had played as a child. Being emotional, Miriam started crying.

In passing she took hold of the arm of Lea, wife of a carpenter from Sepphoris.

"Tell me, Lea, why did they ignore me and not wish me shalom?"

"Because of your son!"

"Because of my son . . . but he is so good! There were people who came up to me to praise me on account of my child."

"He is not good, Miriam."

"How could you say that, Lea? He lives entirely for others. He has never wanted anything for himself."

"They say that he wants the Romans to destroy the Temple."

"Say no more, Lea, chalili li, that cannot be true."

"They say that he mocks the Torah and encourages people to dishonor the Sabbath!"

"Chalili li! That is not true, Lea! I know my son. He loves the Torah and the Sabbath is holy to him. Do you know how much he loves Torah? As a child he once told me that it might not be enough that one wears the words of the Law around the arm and as a sign between the eyes, that one should be able to drill a hole in one's chest so that Torah flows into the heart. Even as a child Yeshua spoke of profound things. He may speak harshly but as his mother I am convinced that he is being slandered. Israel has no better child than he." Then she turned off and walked with bowed head. She remembered the dream she had before he was born, just like the one that Hannah had before Samuel came.

She was filled with joy that she would give a special child to Israel with the blessing of God on his head. Now God's words had come true but she had imagined a different kind of happiness—one without controversy that was not so heavy. A mother is not a partisan like the Sadducees, Pharisees, Zealots and Herodians. She did not want strife to surround her child. Some people claimed that her womb was blessed, something that embarrasses a woman. Others said bad things about her son, things that a Jewish woman did not want to hear. She had hoped that she and her son would live in peace; she never expected them to be elevated between opposing camps. She could not, however, dictate to God what kind of greatness he wished to bestow upon her son.

Miriam had wandered off to ponder these things. Now she joined her friends from Nazareth again.

Rachel could find no rest after she was informed that men were seeking her son. They called him "kelev ha derachim," the stray dog. They did not know to which party he belonged but he was suspected of having had a part in all the unrest against the Romans. Others said that he was a Nazarene that informed Jesus about the plots of his adversaries. It was also said that he—although no "charid," no authority in the Law—was spying for the Pharisees. Rachel knew that he loved their people and only desired to keep Israel united but those who sought him wished to have him arrested. He did not even come around on the eve of Passover. Rachel was afraid that he might have, since her house was being spied on. Fear gripped her heart—had he already been taken by the enemy? Was he dead? She believed that he still had a long life ahead of him but dared not hope that his death was impossible. She lived alone after her husband had left Israel, the tiny nation with a heart so large that one could get lost in it. Both she and her son were lost in it, but where was he?

She donned a dark veil, left the house and headed towards the Temple area with the sounds of singing and feasting in her ears. In the holy area things were quiet except for the occasional sound of a sacrificial animal. What feeling could God have for that? People had a need to offer sacrifices and God is so good. Rachel was the daughter of a man from the School of Hillel—she was brought up in the teaching of God's empathy and tenderness and had taught that to her son.

She passed through a quarter with high walls to a broad street where she saw men and women following a troop of soldiers that was bringing someone to jail. She turned her face away. Then she reached the mountain road from where one could see the palaces of Herod and the murdered

Maccabees. Next, she found herself on the way to Ephrata. The dawn was approaching; she felt exhausted and sat down by the side of the road.

After having rested, she stumbled on again like a very old woman. Three more times she rested and rose again. Finally she saw some camels on a spacious plain that held the grave of her namesake Rachel the matriarch. She thought about Rachel with compassion. The matriarch did not have many children but her two sons Joseph and Benjamin were special. Jacob loved her more through them.

Why was Sarah not considered the mother of the Jews instead of the delicate Rachel? Did the children of Jerusalem expect the children of her time, like her son Menachem and Miriam's son Yeshua? She became calmer as she approached the burial cave. At the entrance stood a woman in blue with a white veil.

The two women recognized each other and were so moved that they embraced and kissed one another on the cheeks.

"Rachel!"

"Miriam!"

"What happened, Miriam, why did you come here?"

"To seek comfort, Rachel, and help for my son Yeshua."

"And you?"

"I also wish to be comforted, Miriam, and want my son Menachem to be protected."

Then Miriam, the mother of Jesus that was so elevated by the people, felt the need to praise another woman. She raised her hands and bowed to Rachel.

"Ashri Rachel, praised be Rachel," she said. "And praised be Menachem, your son of whom it is said in Nazareth that he is a comforter of Israel."

Rachel replied with a mournful smile: "Can Israel be comforted, Miriam?"

Rachel bowed to Miriam of Nazareth, telling her tenderly: "Ashri, Miriam, may you be praised and may your son be praised. They say in Israel that he is the savior of all mankind."

Likewise Miriam smiled sadly:

"Can mankind be saved, Rachel?"

The two women fell into one another's arms from love and a shared anxiety for the destiny of their sons. Then they kneeled, kissed Rachel's gravestone and prayed: "O Mother, protect our sons and give your blessing to your children in Judah and Benjamin! Amen! Amen!"

7

It was a grievous Passover meal. Jesus wished to place events between himself and his fate which could not be avoided anymore. He was afraid that he might wish to escape his destiny. And like a lion tamer, he had tested his lions. "One of you will betray me," he exclaimed. The grim, lean lion Judas with the dark mane roared. The others wanted to know who it was. "The one to whom I give the soaked bread." And Jesus stretched out his hand and the lion Judas leapt up and took the bait. The tamer was satisfied and the lot was cast. The lions liked their Master and like large cats they milled about him to rub their skin against his power and his love. Then they jumped up against him to find out who was the greatest. "Be at peace men, no one is greater than the other, leave that sort of rivalry to kings. You are my lions and no one is greater or smaller than the other." Yet the large, loyal lion Peter started roaring. Jesus put his hand on Peter's head—Peter melted with love and started to lick his Master's hand.

And the human Peter said: "Lord, I am ready to follow you everywhere, into the dungeon and unto death." The Master patted the large lion's head twice and said: "Tsk, tsk, my son. Do not roar with too much loyalty. Before the cock crows this morning, you will deny me three times." The lion Peter groaned with sorrow over these words of unbelief. The lion Judas shot to the front and showed the Master—who made it clear to his lions how well he knew them—his bloodthirsty mouth. And the die was cast. The Master smiled in sorrow about the work that he had accomplished.

"Let's go, sons!"

In the dark Jesus and his men walked to the Mount of Olives not far from the road to Jericho. All joy had left them. The Master, without whom life would lose its meaning, wished to go away. Jesus thought: "If one has to live with the image of death and departure before you, it is better to die. That is the will of God, of Scripture, of the well-being of the people and also of my broken heart." They followed Jesus up the mountain to a deserted garden of trees and shrubs called Gethsemane.

The moon was anchored at one point of its crescent and the stars smeared the heavens with their silver while their rays captured the trees in the nakedness of night. But the shrubs were angry about the remaining light and about the human feet trampling them. Some bowed their grey-green stems and expressionless faces but many pulled their swords to resist the footsteps. However the plants could not do anything about the events that would follow.

Jesus isolated himself in order to pray and to prepare himself for the road ahead. He also prayed for the men that he was about to send out into the world since the lost sheep and the sinners of Israel did not satisfy him anymore. He had ascended the tree of his words and wanted the branches of the treetop to spread around the world.

After having prayed, he returned to his comrades to encourage them for the coming hours. No one, however, knew that Menachem was there too, lying between two mighty cypress trees with his body on their roots and his head in his hands. Furthermore, the apostles had not noticed that Judas Iscariot was missing.

"Why am I so terrified?" Menachem wondered, "and why did I always fear this moment so much? What will now take place? Jesus wishes to be thrown outside like the keys of a besieged citadel. And they will throw him out. Another siege of Jerusalem and another exile are coming. How can the heart of a Jew bear all of this? You will only be crucified once, Yeshua! Think about your people. They were banished to Egypt and Babylon. Can the heart of Israel bear another one? Do not take this road, Yeshua. Do not let yourself be cast out."

A noise was heard and torches lit up the night. The garden's rest was disturbed a second time by a group of men and again the plants bowed their heads or pulled their useless swords. Menachem could not discern whether the approaching men were Jews or Romans. Perhaps a blend of both. Judas Iscariot was in front. He walked up to Jesus and kissed him ecstatically on both cheeks. He felt triumphant that he could show the soldiers and guards how close he was to Jesus of Nazareth. He felt elevated that he could demonstrate to the apostles what weight he carried with the worldly powers. He was happy and proud and bitter. In that moment all his aspirations came together: power other others, admiration from all sides. With his thin arms he had hoisted up his own banner of importance. This was the hour of his triumph and his despair. The devil sat on his heels, small like a poisonous crab. Now the devil sat at his throat with the crowd on both sides looking on.

Jesus looked at him and said; "You betray the son of man with a kiss, Judas." Then the banner became as heavy as a mountain; Judas collapsed under the weight. The men that followed him tried to arrest Jesus but Simon Peter pulled his sword and attacked one of them in the dark, a servant of the high priest. In one swipe he slashed off his right ear.

"Stop that, Simon Peter," Jesus said softly. "He who pulls the sword will perish by the sword."

Menachem, however, did not listen—with his dagger he stabbed one of those who apprehended Jesus.

After Jesus had undermined the idea of just retaliation against the injustice of the world, the apostles became afraid and melted away in all directions.

"Those who believed in you have scattered," thought Menachem, "but he who loves you stays just like a mother does not abandon her child even if it is attacked by a lion."

Menachem followed the solemn procession of soldiers and servants that took Jesus to the palace of Caiaphas, the high priest.

That night many dignitaries and experts of the Law had been summoned to see and judge Jesus. Menachem met his friend Sirach near the palace and pretended to be a student of this member of the Sanhedrin so that he was able to enter the inner court.

"Why all this preening?" Menachem asked Sirach. "The honor belonged to Moshe Rabbinu, not to the tribal chiefs. The mighty and the great do not see the germ. They walk over it. Have ever the learned and the powerful recognized the seed of the time? That was the privilege allotted to Moshe, to David, to Yeshua, to the solitary, the singers and the prophets."

There stood the high priest Caiaphas, large and imposing. Menachem despised him and resented the fact that such a man should judge Yeshua and the people of Israel. He was surrounded by rabbis, scribes and young students. Menachem thought he saw Saul of Tarsus, Mathias bar Yochai and others. They all looked solemn, the younger ones appeared fanatical, and yet they were only after profit. Looking for profit in the Law, looking for profit in oppression, looking for profit in God by explaining who He was and how He was. Oh if they only knew that profit from the Law and profit from God were only human profit, the circling of bees around a flower. Now they will judge Yeshua. And on top of that, Yeshua himself was sending people out with words that would again become stones used for killing people and lures for attracting people looking for profit.

In their midst lies the germ of time and they cannot see it. They did not know what to do with it.

Jesus was made to face Caiaphas who started the interrogation:

"Are you the son of God?"

Yeshua admitted that he was indeed. He stood there in front of the high priest as if held aloft by wind and light.

"And why should he not be, since he's a human being?" Menachem asked himself as the high priest who related God to his position and his denomination, started tearing his overcoat as a sign of shock while exclaiming: "Who said that we needed witnesses to judge this man? You have heard. He has blasphemed the Holy Name. We do not need any witnesses."

Many men bore down on Jesus, pleased to have encountered a blasphemer that they could beat and spit at. They spat in his face and hit him on his arms. He endured it all calmly but asked: "Why are you doing this to me? Have I not performed many miracles in your presence; have I not healed many of your brothers and sisters?"

Some elder Pharisees stepped forward. Abba Alexander was amongst them. His cheeks had sunk and his eyes were filled with sorrow.

"We are not doing that on account of the miracles but because you have blasphemed."

Menachem whispered to Sirach: "Blessed are the poor in spirit for theirs is the Kingdom of God. Sirach, do you think Yeshua can see the innocence in the eyes of these Pharisees? Why does he use their ignorance as a trap?"

"How we would have loved him if he had wanted to be our prophet," said Sirach. "He would have won over the high priest and the entire Sanhedrin. If one is so close to God, why would you wish to be God?"

"It is inexplicable, Sirach, it is inexplicable to all of us and to Yeshua himself. Now we are losing him too. Have we not lost enough of our fruits of which we were not allowed to eat?"

Menachem had gone outside where he sat with his hands around his head, when he heard a woman's voice. She was telling some men that she lived with a smith. A beam projected above the door of the workshop.

When she tried to enter the house earlier that evening, it felt as if someone had kicked her in the stomach. She thought the devil had done it but no, it was a corpse hanging from the beam. She fled in terror and joined the throng at the palace. Menachem got up and walked toward the street that she had mentioned, a narrow street near the palace of the high priest. He found the alleyway that led to the workshop and he saw the body dangling there. It was Judas. His mouth hung open, revealing a purple tongue and black gums. He had died for Jesus by the curse of Jesus.

"Oh," thought Menachem, "instead of the evil, an evildoer has died. It was a good start; Yeshua had summed him up very well. He had observed the evil in Judas, cut away the rest and revealed the inner being. Yeshua had given form to a life. I feel the urge to kiss the accursed Judas Korach that has cast Yeshua and Israel into misery. One can see whatever you want in a face." His head that was leaning to one side looked like that of a dark wolf. But when you bent down and look from below, it looked like a black sheep. He left the body of Judas and returned to the room of the high priest.

A large, bulky figure was stumbling towards the exit, weeping like a child. It was Simon Peter.

"I have denied him, I have failed him, my lord, my friend, Yeshua, Yeshua! Just like he predicted, I denied him three times before the cock crowed. Woe is me, woe is me! They beat him with sticks and he was still praying for me and wanted me to build on his work and use me as the plaster to hold the bricks. I have denied my master and by God, I didn't want to and I did not know that I was capable of it."

Menachem shook his head in empathy, thinking: "What is it about Yeshua that he makes people ashamed? How could I blame him for shaming Pharisees when he has shown his own disciples the sin within them and proved that a man fails until the end?"

He followed Simon Peter as the tenderness welled up in his heart; then he put his hands on his shoulders and kissed him on the cheek from behind.

Peter swung around like a wild horse. "Who are you, who are you, and what do you want? Is it you, unbeliever?"

"Yes, it is I, Simon Peter."

"Don't touch me!"

"You love the kiss of Judas more than that of a friend!"

"You are not alive to me unless I can bring you to Christ."

"Then I'll never be alive in your eyes, Simon Peter. Think about it: you know that dietary laws separate people. I know that your master is no friend of such laws. Yet you must beware, Simon Peter, not to set God himself as a barrier between people. Everyone believes in his own way. Take comfort, Cephas. You may have denied Yeshua tonight but if he had looked at you through my eyes he would never have been so fond of you. A man in his weakness opens himself like a woman that gives birth, bringing new life into the world. That is why your Master loved people in their weakness. May you be blessed, Peter!"

The greater part of the members of the Sanhedrin had decided to deliver Jesus up to the Romans.

This was the second time that they delivered themselves up to the Romans. They had previously involved the Romans in the conflict between Hyrkanus and Aristobulus.

Now they were delivering themselves up in the person of Yeshua. "Yeshua himself stepped out of Israel but an Israel that hands over one of its sons to the Romans also steps out of Israel." And to whom were the temporary powers delivering Yeshua? To Pontius Pilate who had had thousands of Jewish patriots crucified. And there was no prophet to warn: "No treaties with Egypt where your fathers lived in bondage!"

Menachem ended up in the midst of the multitude in the forecourt of the plaza. The proconsul emerged; next to him stood Yeshua between two soldiers. Menachem was shocked by what he saw: Jesus's face was covered in blood.

The Roman, Pontius Pilate, moved forward towards the delegates of the Sanhedrin and said *ECCE HOMO*, "There's the man." And inside Menachem a sad voice said: "They are going to kill a man since he once more tried to be God. When we built the tower of Babel we tried to do that. God foiled that plan. Now this man is on the highest step. They're going to crucify him. Many will believe that the attempt had succeeded but Israel will remain humble because it is chosen. Israel will remain humbly kneeling before God and crying: "Kadosh, Kadosh, Kadosh, Adonai Tzebaoth."

"*ECCE HOMO*," Pilate repeated and sent Jesus to the men of the Sanhedrin. And they sent him back to the Romans.

"*Ecce homo*," said Menachem, "on behalf of God and Rome people are playing chess with the man."

Pilate disappeared. The multitude in front of his palace seemed to be divided. Amongst them there were Nazarenes that cried: "What has he done wrong? He was good to the poor! He performed many miracles! It is even claimed that he raised someone from the dead! A man from Bethany!"

"Yes, Eliazar from Bethany!" another cried.

The defenders of Jesus were mostly from Jerusalem. The Galileans kept quiet in order to avoid being ridiculed for their accent.

Pilate came out again, followed by another man in chains between two soldiers.

Menachem recognized the man as one of Ben Nesher's followers; he seemed to remember that the name was Gershom haYerichi.

"You may choose," shouted the Roman. "It is customary to release one convict on your feast of unleavened bread. Here we have Jesus that I believe is called the king of the Jews. And here is Barabbas the thief. Who do you wish to be pardoned?"

A vague murmur arose in the crowd. Some started calling: "Jesus, give us Jesus!" as it seemed so obvious.

However, a group of students that wanted to know better started shouting: "Give us Barabbas the thief!"

Mathias bar Yochai jumped on a pile of stones. Saul of Tarsus collected people around him to listen. "Choose Barabbas!" shouted Mathias. "He may be a thief that steals your money but Jesus of Nazareth steals our inheritance and our power. What do we know after so many centuries of sin and falling away?: 'Hear O Israel, The Eternal, our God is One!'—and what does the Torah emphasize: 'You will love him with all your might and all your power and all your heart.' Jesus of Nazareth claims that God is not One, that he is His son. He is in the Father, he says, and the Father is in him. He claims that he came to fulfill the Law. I tell you, one of the two is lying! Either God's holy Torah—may my brain rot if I believe that—or this Jesus of Nazareth. Remove him from your midst, lest God's law perish." "Choose Barabbas! Barabbas, give us Barabbas!" shouted the bystanders.

Moving to the group around Saul of Tarsus, Menachem heard him exclaiming: "Who does Jesus love? Who, I ask you? Does he work for the glory of God? He said so once but do you know what he answered the high priest tonight in our presence? That he is like God and will rule the world! Does he work for God? No, he works for himself. Does he work for Israel? He wants to destroy and rebuild the Temple. Israel is supported by the Temple. Our whole land is supported by the Temple. Should it be destroyed, Israel will have no anchor on earth and we would have to wander without support. No, he's a heretic. He wants his own temple. He works for himself. Choose Barabbas!"

"Barabbas, we want Barabbas!" shouted the people around Saul of Tarsus.

"Three times he deliberately broke the laws of Sabbath in order to lead the people astray. And what are we without the Law? Nothing. Manure, to be strewn over other nations and other lands, just like the fate that befell the ten tribes," stated Ruben haCharid to a group of elders. "What did he give us in its place? Things that all of us know—that we must love one another! Does he love us? Did he love us when he made light of a mitzvah? He mocked us about the rule of washing one's hands after having answered the call of nature. We are only Pharisees, dumb, stiff-necked scribes. Does this Yeshua think we do not know that hands that are washed do not mean the soul is pure? The Law is a Law of steps but he that stands on the lowest step is closer to the highest than the one standing on the ground! The one who wants to take the Law from us treats us worse than the Romans that looted the Temple. Elders, you are carrying God's child in your arms—not Yeshua but the Torah. Don't let it fall, so choose Barabbas the thief!" The shout became dominant and only a few Nazarenes were brave enough to keep shouting: "Let Jesus go!"

Menachem could not hold his tongue any longer. He climbed on a pile of stones: "You don't know either of the two! Barabbas is no thief; he was a freedom fighter for Israel. I saw how he liberated your sons who were captured by the Romans, before he was caught. Israel cannot distinguish between its thieves and its heroes anymore. And Jesus of Nazareth is no unbeliever. He poured out his love over you but God did not intend him for you. See how he looks sadly towards the nation he gave his love to and that is being taken away from him. This man is innocent. He gave you all that he had."

"He called himself a son of God."

"Then he must believe it. How do we know what takes place in God's divine presence?"

"That one himself is a Nazarene!"

"Nay."

"Then what are you?"

"A man of Israel, for Israel. A poor shepherd who wishes to protect the flock so that not one sheep is lost."

"He's mad!"

Menachem jumped from the heap of stones and managed to reach the front plaza of the proconsul. A group of rich men were arguing with the Roman:

"You know what this Jesus said, that he was king of the Jews. We do not have a king of the Jews. We recognize only one ruler: Your Caesar, Emperor of Rome!"

Pontius Pilate suppressed a smile in order to appear solemn.

Then Menachem shouted: "Let Jesus go, let Barabbas go and take rather this rich man because he is the type that wishes to kill Israel!"

"Who's that?" the Roman asked one of the notables of Israel near him.

"A rather innocent man, lord, a son from a good house that has become poor."

As Menachem joined the multitude, they were shouting in unison: "Give us Barabbas, give us Barabbas!"

8

MENACHEM ACCOMPANIED HIS FRIEND Yeshua on his final journey. Although very few were interested in the condemned prophet the very best and the very worst of people were amongst them. Some curious folk and some sadists that enjoyed seeing a fellow human being tortured. Some fanatical opponents who wished to gain sustenance from the death of another. Some indifferent individuals who encountered the procession by chance and joined it. Some of the pious, who did not derive joy from the death of Yeshua and were begging God for forgiveness until the last minute as if a sin were taking place. Amongst these was old Abba Alexander, the strict religious teacher who was lifted out of his rigid thinking by a personal experience. How could he know what had to be done to a good man who had questioned the dogma of the oneness of God. How could he be expected to know? He was only a simple Jewish teacher.

There were also some secret followers of Jesus who accompanied their Master. The attractive apostle John—Yochanan and a few women who used to know him from Galilee. And Miriam, his mother from Nazareth, walked in the somber procession; it broke Menachem's heart when he noticed her. Although he was never allowed into the group of disciples, he did experience great things with Yeshua in Israel. He shared his greatest and most beautiful days. Now death approached and afterwards, strange glory would likely follow. Menachem was a witness of these meaningful days.

The Romans had not given Jesus enough to eat so he walked with difficulty, with a human, pained expression on his face. A farmer followed him, carrying his cross.

It was so difficult for Menachem, having to finally part with his friend. He would have preferred to die with Yeshua just like he once wanted to die with Ben Nesher. But the people were needy and could not lose a single man. God and the nations rocked the tree, day and night, summer and winter. Yeshua moaned from thirst and exhaustion and stood still. The soldiers, however, had no mercy and hit him on the knees so he had to proceed.

Why did the journey to Golgotha have to be like this? Every time Jesus had to lift his knees to place his feet on a higher stone, he had to give his whole life over and over again.

And Menachem started to shout but no one heard as it happened within him.

"Oh Yeshua do not do it, fling that cross away from you. Let it be thrown down. If you don't, you will be crucified again and again."

Menachem fell and hurt his knees.

Then he continued to cry out in his soul: "Don't do it Yeshua. They will crucify your people and accuse them of wishing you dead, but you know that in every generation God shakes the peoples and mixes them up."

Jesus groaned: "I am thirsty, give me something to drink!"

A cruel fellow mocked: "The Messiah is thirsty. Can't you change water into wine anymore, Messiah?"

Menachem hit him in the face with his fist: "Today you defame Yeshua and pretend that you're doing it to honor God. And tomorrow you will defame Israel and claim that you're doing it to honor Jesus." The guy cursed Menachem but wouldn't dare return the blow.

And Menachem continued his litany as he climbed the way with Jesus.

"In every generation God shakes the peoples and mixes them up. There are but two nations, Yeshua, Abel's and Cain's. Amongst the children of your friends of today there will be those of Cain. Throw away the cross!"

"I wish that it was done," Jesus sighed. His dry tongue tried to whet his parched lips.

"And amongst the children of your enemies of today there will be those of Abel, Yeshua. Throw way the cross! And always the Cains, your enemies, will fall upon the Abels and crucify them. Why is this suffering necessary? Throw away the cross!"

"Five more high steps," sighed Yeshua on the rough uphill climb.

"And you will know that there will be Cains amongst those who call on your name and friends amongst those who do not call upon your name. Oh Yeshua, Yeshua, do not complete this sacrifice to yourself and to your friends in the far future."

"Five more steps," said Jesus, "then the sacrifice is done."

"Let me share his pain," pleaded Menachem, "since he's doing it for the people."

From two sides swords pierced him and he bowed down like a wounded person, ready to die.

"Take my child Menachem, they are murdering us!" called the voice of a mother. "And save the rest of Israel."

And on the neck of the bowing Menachem fell a child, just like a child was once thrown in his arms.

He climbed one more step. "Four more steps, and then I'm going to my Father," sighed Jesus.

"Father, strengthen me and forgive those that are doing it to me for they do not know what they do."

"Nay, not four, twenty more steps, every step is a whole century," shouted Menachem.

"Take my child!" a father screamed. "They've murdered its mother. I myself wish to die, but save the Shaerith shel Yisrael,[1] Menachem!"

And another child was thrown on the neck of Menachem.

"I'm dying, I'm dying, my God," sighed Menachem. "Will you build a tower on my shoulders of the remnant of Israel?"

They climbed higher still. Jesus who was going to the cross and Menachem, who wished himself to be crucified in Israel.

"One more step." The old look appeared in the eyes of Jesus and the Man once again looked at mankind with reproach, love and conviction.

"Nay, many more steps. I cannot count them anymore," Menachem replied. "I do not even feel our suffering anymore as I am too weary for my weariness."

"Take our child!" a multitude was shouting. "They are murdering us! Save the rest of Israel." And simultaneously, many children fell on Menachem shoulders.

"My God, my God, how heavy Israel is for those who love her," signed Menachem.

They had reached the height of Golgotha and the soldiers proceeded to complete their task.

Golgotha was bare and dry. The palace of Herod lay in the distance and further on, Gehennom, the valley of death. And to the east Jerusalem, towards which Jesus was staring with doubt and intense compassion.

1. The remnant of Israel.

Prophets were chosen for their love of Yerushalayim. When they come down to earth to see the bride, they have to cause her anguish and instead of a wedding, offer her the grave!

The soldiers grabbed hold of him, held him to the cross, spread his arms and drove nails through his hands and then through his feet.

"Woe, woe! Those who tear the flesh of a hand and a foot like that are rending heaven and earth apart!" Menachem called out.

"Shut up, madman!"

Menachem was not aware if he himself were still alive or somewhere else with Yeshua. Time burst asunder. Then he heard a sigh. Jesus raised his eyes and looked at the world like a child. He never looked at his mother like that since he was a man even in his childhood. Now he looked at the world with the eyes of a child, like one of the many children that he had healed.

"Eli, Eli, lama sabachtani,"[2] he said.

"I think he's calling Elijah the Prophet," opined one of those indifferent ones in the crowd.

"If he were Messiah, he would have known to wait for Elijah to arrive before him in order to announce him," observed one young scholar.

"Don't speak like that, my friend," Menachem whispered to Yeshua. "Be strong. Believe now that you are God's only son, then you will be strong and I will be strong for you. But if you call 'lama sabachtani,' then I cannot carry on because then you are a human being and I think of you as tenderly as I remember my mother. Remain strong in your faith my friend, through this terrible suffering."

Then Menachem lost consciousness. Grief hung over him when he woke up, grief about the divide between his friend and his people. He opened his mouth and bit the soil, kissing the dust.

Morning broke over the land. The mount of skulls too, Golgotha, revealed itself to the new day as if it were a flowerbed or a stream. What did the night of Golgotha preserve to donate to the day? There stood three small crosses, not much larger than human beings. Three people were nailed to the dead wood. Two of them were thieves but their flesh was human and nature was affronted. The third was Yeshua, the man from Nazareth. He willed this end himself. Perhaps God had willed it so. But the people had insulted the spirit. One group in Israel did not want God to become flesh. The nations wanted God to taste the misery of a human being and to die

2. "My God, my God, Why hast though forsaken me?" (Psalm 22:2).

like one. All of them knew so well what suited God and what did not. Grief surrounded Golgotha but nature didn't care. The sky above Golgotha was as blue as that over Lake Kinnereth with its lovely flowers and shrubs. The blue sky served willingly as a backdrop to the three hanging humans and to the crows and circling vultures, as it did to the cedars and the pillars of the Temple.

Once more Jesus raised his eyes, despite the fact that virtually everything of flesh and spirit in him was broken. He reminded himself of the world, the cross, his life; then he noticed a woman who was sobbing silently beside his cross. It was his mother. In front of the cross sat a few of his disciples, including Yochanan, the one he loved. Jesus had never acted tenderly towards his mother. Miriam thought he didn't notice her but he did, as he told her: "Woman, go with him!" Then, as the last life was leaving him, he mumbled to the disciple: "This is your mother." Then he gave up the ghost and died too soon.

Menachem lay some distance away on the rocks of Golgotha. When he heard the wailing of the women intensifying, he told himself: "My friend is dead. I am the only one who will stay in Israel and live in the Faith; the only one who does not believe in him yet still mourns him." Again he tore his clothes. The world has become richer and we have become poorer.

We needed the Son of Man as much as the nations needed the Son of God. Yeshua was from Israel but for the nations. The Son of Man that we needed so much, we had to let go.

He rose and reluctantly approached the little group of weary wailing mourners sitting and lying before the cross of Jesus. As Miriam saw him approaching, a feeling of comfort and warmth engulfed her. "Menachem," she called out a welcome to him as if she wanted to throw herself in his embrace. Simon Peter, Thomas and Yochanan surrounded her, pleading: "Do not speak to the man, mother! He's an unbeliever, he rejected your son!"

Their words made Miriam reel but she broke through to Menachem who took both her hands in hers.

"Mariam, Mariam, my heart drags me down," he said, weeping with her. "Menachem, they say I'm not allowed to talk to you. They say you denied Yeshua. You don't believe in him."

"Oh Mariam, what does belief mean? I loved him."

"Am I not permitted to talk to you anymore, Menachem, are you not my Comforter, the son of my people?"

"Oh Mariam, do not say that, even though it is true. The disciples are right; you belong to him, not to me."

"Why, Menachem?"

Softly Menachem replied: "Because such is his will."

"Menachem, are you not my friend anymore, the son of my people?"

"I still am, Miriam, but Yeshua has left Israel and you are his mother."

Lowering her head to her arm, Miriam wept bitterly.

"Do I have to lose Israel too, my own people, the lap in which I live, the garment that warms me?"

"Even that, Miriam, on behalf of your son."

"Shalom, Menachem, son of my people."

Menachem prostrated himself before Miriam, kissing her feet.

"And peace be with you, Mariam."

Watching her return to the disciples with faltering step, he thought of her sincerity, her dedication, her mannerisms and the way she followed Jesus to Golgotha. Overcome with sorrow, Menachem followed her with eyes full of love.

There were pious men in the Faith who believed that a Jew who had died, even by judicial execution or outside of Israel, reverted to the Community of Israel after death and that they ought to care for the body. Amongst these was old Abba Alexander. Together with some other elderly friends and two or three secret supporters of Jesus, he had visited Pontius Pilate and obtained permission to take him down from the cross and give him a proper burial. A wealthy member of the Sanhedrin, Joseph of Arimathea, had already made a burial place available. When they reached the cross, the soldiers asked whether they ought to break the bones of the King of the Jews like they had done with the two criminals. Jesus's friends claimed that it was unnecessary. One soldier, who wanted to make sure, took his spear and pierced the side of the corpse but there was no reaction from the one who had borne the despair of mankind to give them hope.

They took him from the cross and started to wash him whereafter they wrapped him in cloth. Abba Alexander eagerly participated in these activities that he had often performed before because it was a mitzvah. He attempted too much, however, not noticing the pain in his chest. He had come to love Jesus like the Father loved the Prodigal Son. Abba did not know the tale but Jesus had once told it to a great multitude. Abba's hands were hasty and eager to get Yeshua, the son of Israel, away from the Romans and back to his own community. It was with too much love that he bent and wrapped the body. As he bent the last time in order to wrap Jesus's face, the bystanders heard a drawn-out, sucking sound. The old Pharisee fell over dead, his head touching the toes of Jesus's feet. Menachem watched the body with compassion. He realized that Abba's daughter was now utterly alone. And the dead one too, since his daughter had fled long before his death.

Slowly Yocheved approached the stone which sealed the burial chamber. Her face was pale and she wore a black veil. Yocheved bent her knees and prayed for the soul of the young Master.

There were some faithful men and women laying and sitting about. Even Menachem lingered there though not for long as his journey with Jesus had come to an end, like his journey with Ben Nesher.

He tapped Yocheved on the shoulder: "Yocheved, your father was taken home. I am afraid that he won't be with us much longer."

"I know," she replied.

"Your father has died, Yocheved."

"I know. What does it matter? When you are drowning you don't notice any particular wave. This is the sea, this is death." She lay her head on the stone sealing the grave.

"You ought to love your father more, not less! The suffering of Yeshua does not mean that the suffering of others does not count, Yocheved."

She rose: "Menachem, I came looking for you. Do you want to take me with you?"

"And him?" asked Menachem, pointing at the grave.

"I love you, do you want to take me with you?"

"I stand with Israel."

"I shall love Israel because you do."

"It is not about me but about loving Israel for itself."

"Israel, Israel, always Israel. Why does the nation mean so much to you?"

Menachem was silent. Then he sighed. "Oh Yocheved, the nation of Israel sits, like Job, on a dunghill. And my words differ from those of Yeshua: 'To those from whom much is taken, much comfort must be given.' You cannot go with me, Yocheved, because you are already in Yeshua, not in Israel. I cannot receive and keep your soul the way Yeshua can. Your measure of grief is full, pour it out in the scale that never fills up. Yeshua came for you. You consider your soul! I remain in Israel for I know terrible times are coming."

"Menachem, you do not want me?"

"I give you to him, the one you have chosen, Yocheved."

"Then I shall follow Yeshua, Menachem, but I agree, they are coming."

Yocheved had brought Baruch with her, the son of the unknown woman that threw him into his arms. He approached; he looked brave with his black hair and honest, open face.

"I brought him up for you, the son of an unknown woman in Israel. Here's your father, Baruch, go with him!"

The boy hesitated.

Once more, Menachem spoke to Yocheved. She was beautiful and he loved her. But she loved her own soul more than being one of the chosen.

"Blessed are those who go, Yocheved. Peace be with you."

Her gaze projected all her love for him.

"Blessed is he who stays, Menachem. Shalom, shalom!"

She walked weeping towards the group of women and disciples at the gravesite.

Hesitantly approaching Menachem, Baruch asked: "Are you taking me with you, father?"

Menachem put his hand on the youth's shoulder. His eyes swept over the depressing Golgotha and west into the distance, towards the wide fertile fields, the shoreline and the sea.

"It will be difficult for one who lived in the fields with Yeshua to go and live with Pharisees in besieged fortresses, Baruch, but it would be even worse for one who lived with Yeshua in the fields to see fortresses being built in his name," he said thoughtfully.

"Come Baruch, let's go back to the city of Israel. We'll return to the heart. That is what I have been living for."

Baruch lay his hand on the arm of his adopted father and asked if Menachem were the Messiah.

Menachem smiled. "The Messiah, my boy, will never come. Many Messiahs will come."

"Then who are you, father?"

"I don't know. Maybe I'm a witness, son, who must witness for his nation. There will always be a witness, Baruch, but I do not know who will be the one after me. I hope you may be the one."

Silently they strode towards Jerusalem.

Again Baruch spoke:

"Father, why are you letting my mother go away by herself?"

"She needs a savior, Baruch, a savior for herself and that I cannot be for her."

Once more the youth asked:

"Father, why are you leaving my mother alone?"

"Because she loves not Israel enough, Baruch."

Jerusalem with all its districts lay before them. Menachem wished to be taken up by the city. He took Baruch's hand, saying: "Your mother lives not in our chosen role, Baruch, she lives for her soul and offers her soul to Yeshua to live as a chosen servant. Listen, son, I want to tell you why a child of Israel must love Israel so much. Other nations are not allowed to love themselves so much, so that they do not sin against their neighbors too severely. Thus the Babylonians, Greeks and Romans have sinned against us and treated us inhumanly. And many nations that love themselves too much and other nations not enough, will do it also.

Israel is chosen. That is why God must afflict us so severely. We must bear the sins of the nations. Here—he looked back and cast a sad glance over the barren Golgotha—Israel has borne again." Menachem continued: "God gives us much so that we may pass it on. At his time He gave us Yeshua and took him away again. He takes much from us but leaves us more. He lets our chosenness weigh heavily upon us so that we know that He stays close by. But because the chosenness hurts and brings pain He commands his children in Israel: 'Love Israel in a way that no other nation may love itself. Remember, she is your mother and she suffers for me!' Of you my son, I expect that you love and protect your mother with all your might and all your power and all your abilities. That is God's command to his sons in Israel. Many do not hear it and do not understand it. Therefore, in every generation God seeks out men in Israel that will love Israel so much so that their mother will not die because she is deserted by her children. I have received the command to be a son like that. And those who wish to keep the nation together and comfort her will also be greatly comforted. You see, from those who love Israel so much, the chosenness shines out and warms just like a mother warms her shivering child. I yearn for my city, Baruch, I yearn for my people, even now that it has lost Yeshua and awaits new burdens. Soon Jerusalem will embrace us!"

Brussels, June 1947

www.ingramcontent.com/pod-product-compliance
Lightning Source LLC
Chambersburg PA
CBHW070303040726
47505CB00020B/1893